ABOUT THIS BOOK

Every town has stories of its past, and Havenwood Falls is no different. And when the town's residents include a variety of supernatural creatures, those historical tales often become Legends. This is but one . . .

For eighteen years, Nathan Wade has searched for answers regarding his father's disappearance. Now, in 1920, he receives a letter from Calla Lily Mircea saying she's in possession of some of his father's belongings in a town called Havenwood Falls. Nathan wonders how a field camera lost on an archeological dig in Egypt could end up in a small town in Colorado, but something draws him in. Nathan takes the leap of faith, only to have his world turned upside down when he finds not only the camera, but a hidden treasure within.

Amani lost everything the day she came of age and her true nature was revealed. Now, having been trapped for eighteen years, her only hope is that someone will save her from the hell she's had to endure. When a handsome stranger inadvertently releases her, the wait is over, and the truth of her imprisonment comes to light.

Nathan and Amani are now bound to one another and determined to piece together the past. Someone wanted her gone, and she and Nathan race to solve the mystery that connects them both before it's too late.

LEGENDS OF HAVENWOOD FALLS BOOKS

Also try the main Havenwood Falls series; the YA line, Havenwood Falls High; the darker, sexier side of town, Havenwood Falls Sin & Silk; and the local supernatural college, Sun & Moon Academy.

Stay up to date at www.HavenwoodFalls.com

ALSO BY BRYNN MYERS

The Prophecies of The Nine Series

Entasy Book 1

Redemption Book 2

The Jorja Graham Duology

The Life & Death of Jorja Graham

The Echoed Life of Jorja Graham

Falling Out of Focus

Captivated by Crimson

Fairytale Confessions—print only

One Last Con—e-book only

TRAPPED WITHIN A WISH

A LEGENDS OF HAVENWOOD FALLS NOVELLA

BRYNN MYERS

CHAPTER 1

The hallway of New York University bustled with students roaming around—some were on their way to exams, while others were chatting about the upcoming summer break.

In his office on campus, Nathan Wade rifled through term papers, trying to find a student's dissertation on the 42 Laws of Ma'at when the door to his office opened, startling him.

"Is this what you've been waiting for?" Lillian asked as she entered the room.

"I don't know, Ms. Hartman. What is it?" Nathan replied as he continued to shuffle through the stack of papers in his hands.

"Enough with that formal business, young man. There are no students around," Lillian scoffed as she wagged the paper she held in the air. "This came in about an hour and a half ago, but you were teaching, and I didn't think it was important enough to interrupt the class to give it to you," she replied with a sly grin. "And why is he sending telegraphs anyway? Has he forgotten we're in the twentieth century? It is 1920, after all."

Nathan shook his head and chuckled under his breath. "What did Edgar have to say with his antiquated form of communication?"

Lillian reached for the silver chain holding her cheaters and pulled them on to see the words clearer. She read the two words and clicked her tongue in frustration. "Nothing yet."

"Nothing yet, what?"

"That's it. That's all it says." Lillian walked over to her desk and sat down. "I do not know why you continue to pay him to look for your father's satchel—it and the camera are long gone." She shook her head slowly. "I'm sorry. I know that is not what you want to hear, but it's true. It's been eighteen years, son. You have to move past this." Her tone shifted from judgmental to soft as she took off her glasses and let them hang around her neck.

"I can't stop searching and you know why," Nathan said as he stared into the eyes of the woman who'd cared for him after his father's disappearance.

Lillian Hartman was widowed, like his father had been. Before Nathan was born, Lillian and her husband, Charles, had been neighbors and close friends with his parents. When Nathan's mother died of consumption, Lillian became Nathan's surrogate mother. Then, after his father disappeared, she and Charles raised Nathan—gave him a life in lieu of his loss.

When Charles passed away a few years ago, Lillian was in need of a hobby to keep her mind busy. All that unused energy was going to waste, and Nathan was in need of an office assistant, now that he was an associate professor at the university. Lillian was the perfect assistant and the most qualified candidate to manage all of Nathan's pastimes.

"Nathan," Lillian soothed, "the clue to where your father disappeared to is not in that camera. Edgar can search the world over and still conclude what we already know. Sam and the camera are gone."

"I want to know what happened, Lillian. Not knowing is what binds me to this quest."

"But some mysteries will never be unraveled. You simply have to move on."

Nathan bowed his head and whispered, "I know."

"You're better suited spending your energy uncovering the mysteries found in those Egyptian tombs you love so much." She grinned and then threw her hands in the air. "That reminds me. I received notification from Howard Carter's office about an expedition opportunity. I'm not certain how that will work with your current class schedule, though."

Nathan glanced up. "They requested me?"

"Yes," she said, handing him the letter. "Here, read it. It's very complimentary."

"Wow, I didn't expect that," Nathan said as he put on his glasses to read the letter. When he read the last line, he grinned appreciatively. "It is indeed very complimentary, but sadly, I'm going to have to pass on this offer and use my time here to study linguistics in my off time." He sighed. "Maybe they'll ask again, for another dig. I can't imagine there won't be more to come."

"Always wanting to learn more. You always were such a curious boy."

"I received word that new funerary texts have arrived at the Metropolitan Museum of Art. They'll need to be translated, and as you have pointed out, it may do me some good to dive into a distraction."

Lillian picked up a stack of mail from the inbox on the corner of her desk and started to flip through it. As she did, she pulled her glasses back on and examined one envelope with an odd symbol pressed into a wax seal.

"Who uses letter seals anymore?" she mumbled under her breath. "Well, I guess whoever this is from," Lillian said to herself as she reached for her letter opener.

Lillian pulled out the neatly folded letter and read the words, disbelief and shock contorting her face with each word she read.

Dear Mr. Wade,

I'm writing this letter to inform you I am in possession of a camera I believe belongs to you. Inside the top flap of the tattered brown leather case is a tag with this New York address. The inscription reads, Samuel N. Wade. I do hope I've not contacted the wrong person in error and that this field camera indeed belongs to you. When you receive this, please reply to the address listed on the envelope.

Sincerely,
Calla Lily Mircea

"What's wrong, Lillian?" Nathan asked.

"Someone in," she paused to flip over the envelope, "Havenwood Falls has found your father's camera. They even have the bag," Lillian muttered. "I can't believe it."

"Where is Havenwood Falls?"

"According to the postage mark, it's someplace in Colorado."

"Colorado?" Nathan exclaimed. "How in the hell did the camera get there? It has to be a mistake. Egypt to some random place in the middle of nowhere is a bit of a stretch, don't you think?"

Lillian nodded, still trying to comprehend the words she'd just read. Sam's camera had been missing for as long as he had been, and no one, besides Nathan, thought they'd ever see it again. She eyed him over her glasses. "Nathan, I don't want you to get your hopes up."

Nathan took the letter from Lillian and stared at the words on the page for a moment before responding. "It may be nothing, but this is the first lead we've had. I will have to contact this Calla Lily and find out for myself."

"No, you can send Edgar. That is why you hired him, is it not?"

Nathan sighed. "It is, but there is something odd about this letter—this woman's writing. I feel like this is it. This," Nathan paused, "this is my father's camera, Lillian. I have to do this."

"Oh, Nathan," she replied gently.

"Look, it won't hurt anyone. Only another week and classes will be out for summer break. I can go then, and that way nothing will be affected here."

Lillian laid her hand on Nathan's. "This could indeed be a mistake, but I understand what you're saying. I will cover you here. I want you to have peace of mind, and I need you to find closure and put your father's death behind you."

"What if it is his? What if he is alive and has been living in Colorado all this time?"

She pulled him into a hug. "Then I guess that is all the more reason for you to go," she said as she stepped back. "Either way, you'll have an answer."

Nathan nodded. "I don't know, Lillian. I have a feeling I can't shake."

"Well, then let me respond to this Miss Mircea and make the arrangements for you to stay a few days," she said, before she kissed him on the forehead and walked over to her desk.

"This had better not be another dead end," Nathan mumbled under his breath as the gentle clicks of the typewriter sounded in the background.

CHAPTER 2

*T*he week passed by quickly, and Nathan was almost ready to go. Lillian had made all the arrangements with Calla Lily for Nathan to stay at Whisper Falls Inn upon his arrival. She also made sure Nathan's colleagues were aware he'd only be gone a short period of time on a fact-finding mission and would be back before summer's end at the latest.

Lillian thought back to when Samuel disappeared. He'd been working at the excavation site for Hatshepsut's tomb in the Valley of the Kings. Everything was going as expected according to his correspondence, and then one day they received a telegraph stating he'd gone missing—simply vanished, no trace of him found by the other Egyptologists on the dig. The only evidence they had was from a worker who reported seeing him taking a photograph of two young women near the excavation site.

Nathan had convinced himself that his father's satchel was the key to finding out what happened. He'd go on and on about photos, or maybe something Samuel found, and how it could show not only inside information about the tomb, but could also provide clues as to what happened on that day. Either way, Lillian worried about how all of this would affect Nathan in the end. Not knowing left him sad, but hungry for information—a conclusion could leave him broken.

Lillian hoped this trip to Havenwood Falls would confirm the final piece of the puzzle and finally let Nathan accept the truth—Sam met with foul play that fateful day, and the camera and any other belongings were long gone from this world. She typed up the last page for the itinerary and slipped it out of the typewriter wheel with a zing, placing it neatly on her desk. As soon as Nathan returned from afternoon class, she'd let him know the whos, whats, and whens for his departure tomorrow.

The door opened with a click and startled Lillian.

"Finished," Nathan called out as he entered the office. "The only thing left to do is mark the grades and submit them, then it's off to Colorado."

"I've made the final arrangements," she said as she stood. "You'll be taking the train into Montrose, Colorado, and Miss Mircea will meet you there. Apparently, they don't have direct access other than a bus to take you into the town itself, so she's offered to be your means of transportation."

Nathan gave her an odd look.

"Yes, my thoughts exactly, but considering your insistence that you yourself flesh this one out, you will have to abide by the rules set forth by the woman who has the satchel," Lillian said with a slight grin.

"Then I shall take it all at face value," Nathan replied, returning her smile. "Did she say where to meet her?"

"No, only that she'd be there when the train arrived, and she'd be on a bench near the platform."

"Okay then," he sighed.

"Have you finished packing?" Lillian asked as she began to sort the papers Nathan had set on her desk.

"Oh you know, I still have a few things to pack," he replied shyly.

"Nathan Allan Wade. I swear, will you never change?" Lillian laughed out loud. "Go home and get packed this instant."

Nathan grinned, knowing his truth was revealed. He hadn't packed a thing, but he was only going to be gone a few days. Nathan didn't see the point in bringing his dress attire. Instead, he'd settle for his field clothes: a couple of sport shirts, casual trousers, and a pair of suspenders.

"I don't have that much . . ." He relented under Lillian's motherly gaze.

"Nonetheless, off you go," Lillian said, shooing him out the door. "And don't forget to stop by the bank on the way home. You should have plenty of cash with you—enough to last the week at least."

"How about dinner tonight at six at Lombardi's?" Nathan asked as he grabbed his coat and hat.

"That sounds lovely, but only if you've done as I've asked and will be ready to leave in the morning. Your train departs at seven, and you cannot be late," Lillian chided.

"I will not only be ready to leave but will have my bags by the door." Nathan grinned. "I'll pick you up at five thirty," he said as he opened the door to leave.

"Five thirty it is." Lillian waved him out.

Nathan stopped by the bank, as Lillian suggested, and then the library. He needed to grab a book or two to keep his mind occupied on the train. It was, after all, going to take a few days to get to Colorado.

It was five thirty sharp when Nathan knocked on the door of Lillian's apartment. She was always a stickler for being on time, and Nathan knew if he was late, she'd balk over needing to rush to dinner. He adored Lillian and wanted nothing more than to make her happy. They lived in separate apartments, but within the same building. Lillian lived on the floor below his, and as they headed down the stairs, Nathan remembered carrying his father's satchel clumsily down each flight before his dad left for his latest expedition. He'd set it down on the last step and taken Lillian's hand as Samuel told her when he'd be returning. That was the last time he saw his father. It was also the day Lillian became his guardian.

"I want you to order whatever you like tonight, and no scrimping because you're worried about the cost, understand?" Nathan insisted.

"Oh no, you will not," Lillian scolded. "We're going to have a lovely dinner, but it will be on me." Nathan started to protest but stopped when she gave him "the look." "Besides, if you pay, I will assume it is to say goodbye, and I will not be saying goodbye to you, young man. You'll return in a week, and when you do, you can buy dinner then." She winked.

"Deal," Nathan replied as he raised his arm in the air to hail a cab.

"We can walk, Nathan."

"I didn't want you to have to walk all that way," he replied as the car pulled up to the curb. "And you gave no stipulation about a taxi, only dinner."

Nathan opened the door and offered his hand to her.

Lillian clicked her tongue, but didn't argue. Instead, the two rode to the restaurant, enjoyed a lovely meal, and returned home early enough for her to be able to read a chapter in her book before heading to bed. Nathan had left before on excursions, but he always came home. Something about him leaving this time felt different, though. They hugged one another tightly as they said their goodbyes.

"Don't worry. I'll be home in a week," Nathan insisted as he kissed her forehead. "I love you, Lillian."

"I love you too, Nathan. Now be careful. I'll hold the fort down here until you return."

He smiled. "You always do."

Nathan looked back one last time before he headed upstairs.

NATHAN SLEPT for most of his three-day trip. The gentle sway of the train and clatter of the wheels on the track lulled him to sleep. When the train pulled into the station, he gathered his things and headed toward the exit. He was anxious, and not because he hadn't traveled before, but because he was not simply venturing into the unknown, but into his own *personal* unknown. What if he found more than just his father's satchel? Then again, what if it was a fake, a trick of some sort? Nathan quickly dismissed both lines of thinking, because it was pointless. Why would someone in Colorado play a joke on a professor in New York? It made no sense.

As he stepped onto the platform, Nathan glanced around, hoping to find a sign saying Havenwood Falls or a woman sitting on a bench waving her hand in the air, but there was nothing—no reference and no woman.

"Excuse me," Nathan asked the conductor. "Which way to Havenwood Falls?"

The man stared at him with an odd expression. "I have no idea where that is, sir. This is Montrose, Colorado. Maybe you should check with the office," he said, pointing to a window in the main building off the platform.

Nathan was confused, but thanked the man and headed in the direction the conductor pointed. He knew this was Montrose, but assumed Havenwood Falls was a town nearby. Why did the conductor act like he'd never heard of it?

"Mr. Wade?"

Nathan turned to see a young woman offering her hand to him. He gave her an odd look, but shook her hand anyway.

"Let me guess, you expected someone older?" she said.

"Ah! Miss Mircea. Actually, I did. I apologize. I meant no offense."

"None taken. Glad to see you made it here safely," she replied with a slight nod. "And please call me Calla Lily."

"What a beautiful name."

"Thank you." She smiled kindly. "This way, we're right over here." Calla Lily pointed to a Ford Model T that had been retrofitted with tires thicker than the norm, obviously a necessity for dealing with the Colorado terrain.

Nathan deposited his bag in the back and climbed inside, choosing to stick to a generic topic like the weather as a way to pass the time while Calla Lily navigated the mountain pass. He was, of course, bursting at the seams to ask all the questions pooling on the tip of his tongue. How had his father's camera ended up in Colorado? Did she remember who brought it in? Did she perhaps see his father firsthand? But, remembering Lillian's words, he wasn't ready to have his hopes crushed just yet, so he'd wait—wait until he saw it with his own eyes before broaching the sensitive subject.

"So, are all the mountain towns around here this hard to find?" Nathan asked as they rounded yet another bend in the road.

Calla Lily stifled a laugh. "No, probably not. Our little town is . . . special, a hidden gem, and we wouldn't have it any other way.

Nathan arched his brow, but dismissed her comment. Instead, he turned back to the window and glanced up at the snow-tipped mountain caps.

CHAPTER 3

*N*athan saw a large wooden sign atop a solid stone base that read "Havenwood Falls" as they entered the town. It wasn't what he expected, but then again, this was the country, and he was a city boy. It was late afternoon when they rolled up to Whisper Falls Inn—a large Victorian-style manor complete with a wraparound porch, turrets and gingerbread trim. He definitely wasn't in New York anymore. The next few days would be slow, easy country living, and for a brief moment, he allowed himself to take in the calm, cool mountain air.

"You coming?" Calla Lily asked as she stepped onto the porch.

Nathan nodded. "Of course. Sorry. Was just taking in the fresh, clean air. Not something I'm used to, I'm afraid."

"Well, there is plenty for you to enjoy while you're here," Calla Lily said as she stepped inside the doorway.

"Nathan, this is Mihail Petran. He and his wife Irina run the inn," Calla Lily said with a bright smile as they made their way to the front desk.

Nathan nodded and extended his hand. "Mr. Petran, it's a pleasure to meet you."

Mihail gave Calla Lily a quick glance before extending his hand in return. Nathan looked between them and dismissed whatever silent conversation they were having.

"A woman named Lillian Hartman made the reservations for me," he said, pulling a slip of paper from his pocket.

Mihail trailed his finger over the guestbook until he found Nathan's name. "Mr. Wade?"

"See," Calla Lily lilted, "everything is as it should be. They'll get you checked in, and I will be back in a bit with the camera, if that works for you?" she said as she touched Nathan's shoulder. "I know you want answers," Calla Lily said softly. "And soon, you shall have them."

Nathan started to speak, but Calla Lily seemed to be out the door before he could gather the first question he wanted to ask her. He'd waited this long, though, so what were a few more hours in the grand scheme of things?

"I have you all checked in, Mr. Wade," Mihail said with a smile. "Irina will show you to your room, and if you need anything while you are here, please do not hesitate to find one of us."

"Thank you, Mr. Petran."

"Please, call me Mihail."

Nathan nodded, but was confused by the sudden chill he felt as he looked at Mihail's eyes—grey-green with an oddly handsome intrigue behind them.

"This way, Mr. Wade," a woman's voice spoke from over his shoulder.

Nathan turned and came face to face with a woman with the same grey-green eyes as Mihail's. He stared for longer than a man should, before apologizing to her profusely. "I'm so very sorry. I was taken aback by your eyes."

"No need to apologize, Mr. Wade. My name is Irina, and I'll be showing you to your room."

"O-of course," Nathan stuttered as he reached for his bag and glanced back at Mihail, embarrassed for staring at the man's wife. "Thank you. Thank you both."

Mihail grinned slightly at Nathan before the professor moved to follow Irina down the hall. When the two of them arrived at his room, Irina opened and held the door for him.

The room was spacious, larger than any he was used to in New York. People often joked that hotels and apartments were postage-stamp-sized unless you were fortunate enough to be wealthy and could afford a larger space. Either way, Nathan was pleased with this room and happy to have the space to spread out. Maybe he'd view this as a vacation after all.

"If you need anything, Mr. Wade, please feel free to call down. We'll be happy to help. Oh, and while we are working on putting a bathroom in each room, yours does not have one yet. The communal bathroom is down the hall to the right. We only have a few guests staying currently, so this floor should be relatively empty. At least that should give you a little peace and quiet while you're here."

"Thank you, Mrs. Petran."

"Madame Luiza serves dinner in the dining room promptly at six. I'll expect to see you in half an hour," she said with a smile before closing the door.

Nathan grinned and thought of Lillian. She, too, was always concerned with whether or not he was properly fed. His stomach growled as he glanced at his watch. It had been a long trip, and while he'd eaten on the train, that had been hours ago. He opened up his bag and grabbed a few toiletries before heading down the hall to wash up.

Nathan stared at his reflection and sighed. He was only twenty-six, but with the circles darkening under his eyes, he appeared much older. The quest to find the answers surrounding his father's death had taken its toll on him. He knew Lillian had seen it, but she always danced around the topic. Yet now, as he looked at himself, so close to the end of this quest, Nathan realized that no matter what he uncovered, he would have to move beyond this. He needed to put his father's death in the past and move forward with his life. When his mother died of consumption, he was too young to have any memories of her, but with Samuel, he had eight years of laughter and fun. All not easily forgotten. Especially when there were no reasons why. Nathan washed his face and tamed the wild hairs on his five o'clock shadow before heading back to his room.

The smell wafting down the hall was too tempting, and Nathan decided to arrive a few minutes early. Irina's mouth curved into a smile when she caught his eye, and he gave her an approving nod as he found a seat and put a napkin into his lap. Nathan thought about Lillian when "Regretful Blues" started to play on the Victrola. It had only been a few days, but he missed her and this was one of her favorite songs.

"Good evening, Nathan," a woman with salt-and-pepper hair and elegant features said as she set down a loaf of bread and a few pats of butter. "We have two dishes this evening, if you're hungry," she lilted. "Pot roast with potatoes, carrots, and onions, or meatloaf and mashed potatoes."

Nathan knew immediately. "Pot roast, please, with extra gravy if you have it to spare."

She laughed. "Extra gravy it is."

"Thank you, Madame Luiza," Nathan replied.

"Ah, a perceptive one. How did you know I was Madame Luiza?"

"I just assumed." He grinned as he reached for a piece of bread.

She winked and turned to leave. "Calla Lily will be joining you shortly, if you care to wait."

Nathan pulled back his hand and set them in his lap, confused as to how Madame Luiza knew he was about to grab the bread with her back turned. A moment later, Calla Lily stepped into the foyer. Nathan saw her talking to Mihail and Irina before turning toward the dining hall. He could see underneath the evening cloak she was wearing that she brought the satchel. *Moments from the truth,* Nathan thought, standing as Calla Lily drew near.

"Calla Lily," Nathan said as he pulled out the chair next to his. "Madame Luiza said you'd be arriving shortly. It seems she was correct."

Calla Lily grinned as she moved to sit, setting the bag next to the chair. "She does have a keen sense when it comes to timing."

Madame Luiza walked in, carrying a tray of teacups and a small teapot. "I assumed you'd want your usual green tea, but I added a bit of passion fruit and mango to it."

She removed the items from the tray and placed them in front of Calla Lily.

"That sounds magnificent, Madame Luiza. I cannot wait to try it, and the pot roast smells heavenly. May I have some of that as well?"

Madame Luiza nodded her head gently. "Two pot roast plates, one with extra gravy, coming right up."

As Madame Luiza made her way to the kitchen, Nathan stole a glance at the bag sitting next to Calla Lily.

"I know you are anxious to see this bag, but I'd like to share a meal —talk and get to know one another—first," Calla Lily said as she laid her hand on his. "Will that be okay?"

"I didn't mean to be obvious. It has been a long time of wanting to know the truth."

"You know, when I saw you this morning, you weren't the only one who was expecting someone older. When I sent the letter, I didn't know who the satchel or camera belonged to, but as I sit here before you, I am curious to know why it means so much."

Nathan sat back in his chair and wondered why it felt as though Calla Lily could see parts in him that he desperately tried to keep hidden. Her caring, soulful eyes seemed to almost draw out the words.

"It's a simple story, but nonetheless a painful one," he started. "My father, Samuel Wade, the man whose bag you have there, was an Egyptologist—a great one, in fact. He was on a dig for Hatshepsut's tomb in the Valley of the Kings when he disappeared—he and the camera. No one has seen either since."

"And you've been searching now for how long?"

"Eighteen years."

"Hope you two are hungry," Madame Luiza said, setting their plates in front of them. "I put a little extra for each of you. And save room for dessert."

Nathan and Calla Lily inhaled and let the scent of the roast tease their senses.

"Thank you very much, Madame Luiza. It looks delicious."

"Enjoy. I'll be back around in a bit to check on you."

"By the way, Madame Luiza, the tea is delicious." Calla Lily beamed. "I believe I have a new favorite."

Madame Luiza laughed. "You say that every time."

When she left, Nathan and Calla Lily ate and chatted, but left the conversation about Sam on hold to enjoy their meals. When they were finished, Madame Luiza refreshed their drinks and cleared their plates before leaving them once again to grab two bowls of homemade cobbler—another one of her specialties.

"So, you've been searching eighteen years for answers to why your father went missing, and you're hoping this bag," she said as she lifted it and set it on the table, "will give you those answers, yes?"

"I do," Nathan replied with conviction.

"Then please promise me you'll look at this as an opportunity for peace. I think you've earned it after all this time, have you not?"

He stared at Calla Lily. "You sound like Lillian."

"Just remember, sometimes the answers you seek don't always come the way you hope. You may find something entirely different. Either way, keep your mind open to the possibilities that may be beyond your understanding." She laid her hand on his. "I only hope for your peace, Nathan."

"Thank you, but if you don't mind me asking, why would *you* be concerned with my peace? You don't even know me."

She scooted out her chair to leave, bringing Nathan quickly to his feet to assist her.

"If you should need anything while you are here in Havenwood Falls, my shop is down the street. Mihail, Irina, or Madame Luiza can show you. Otherwise, I wish you well," Calla Lily said, extending her hand.

Nathan was taken aback as to why she didn't reply, but assumed it was because their business was unofficially concluded. "I will make certain before I leave town to find you and let you know what, if anything, I have found. It has been a great pleasure meeting you."

"And you also. Be well."

Nathan watched as Calla Lily retrieved her coat and made her way to the door. When she was out of sight, he sat and stared at the bag. He ran his hands over the supple leather, but flinched when a spark ran up his arm.

"Everything okay?" Madame Luiza asked.

"Yes," Nathan stammered. "I'd like to pay my bill, please."

Madame Luiza shook her head. "No bill. Dinner is served with your stay. If you get hungry later, and are looking for leftovers, we're up late around here. Just come on down, and we'll fix you a plate."

"You're too kind."

"Have a good evening."

"You as well."

Nathan reluctantly reached for the bag but was surprised when it didn't shock him this time. He made his way upstairs, and when he got to his room, he set the satchel on the dresser. All this time, and now he didn't want to open it. *What's another day?* he thought.

CHAPTER 4

*N*athan lay in the bed, staring across the dimly lit room at the satchel. He wanted to open it, but feared the truth, now that it was here within his reach. He rubbed his fingers together, remembering the shock it had given him. Was that part of the reason why his father was missing, or was it the altitude and dry air here in the mountains? *Get up and open it, you idiot. All the answers you seek are right there. But what if . . . what if what?* His internal debate raged until he finally sat up with a renewed determination. Nathan reached over and turned on the lamp on the nightstand, before deciding to settle this once and for all. He stepped over to the dresser and picked up the bag.

With the light beaming on the satchel, Nathan ran his hands over his father's name, and when he didn't feel a shock, he opened it slowly. Inside, it was like a time capsule of Samuel's life. Nathan knew in an instant this was indeed his father's bag. He pulled out a leather-bound journal and set it on the bed, followed by a stack of pictures from the dig, dated in his handwriting days before his disappearance. Nathan removed the elastic band on the stack and flipped through them. They were nothing more than images of artifacts and some of the other Egyptologists posing with their finds.

He then unwrapped the leather strap on the journal and opened it.

Tears came to his eyes. There on the first page was the last photograph of him and his father together before Samuel had left for Egypt. Snow covered the ground, and they were sitting on a sled. He remembered the day vividly. They'd had fun going up and down the hills near the cabin they'd been staying at in the Catskills. Nathan was sad but grateful to have it back. Samuel was only supposed to have been away for three months when he'd left. No one could have ever predicted it would've been the last vacation they'd have together.

Nathan flipped through the journal pages, but nothing stood out. There were field notes and scaled drawings, along with slips of paper with hieroglyphics sketched onto them. Everything in there, besides the photograph of him and his father, was related to his work. Nathan flipped to the center, where the binding of the journal was broken and the pages lay flat, exposing a detailed description of a canopic jar unlike anything he'd ever seen.

Notation: Most jars are cylindrical and between five to ten inches tall and range in material based on the wealth of the owner whose remains are inside. This one is different. It appears to be two jars connected as one, while still maintaining its individual shape. It is made of alabaster with ribbons of red and orange running through it and stands nineteen and a half inches tall.

Nathan read his father's notes and wondered, just as he had, why such a jar would exist. When it was found, it was sitting on a ledge with a dozen or so red stones carved like scarabs and a shimmering liquid no one could identify. Nathan ran his fingers over the ancient symbols to the right of the page. They were unlike anything he'd ever seen. He wondered if maybe they were the key to explaining the jars and the mysterious liquid. Nathan scanned the next few pages, hoping they'd provide some insight, but found nothing. He closed the journal and decided he'd research this later, after he returned to New York, where he had the resources to uncover more information.

Nathan reached into the bag again, this time taking great care when lifting the field camera out. It was lighter than he remembered, but then again, he was a boy the last time he'd had his hands on it. He set it on the bed and stared at it a moment before something at the bottom of the bag caught his eye—a stack of aged images scattered across the bottom. Nathan moved to pick them up, but flinched when he got another shock, similar to the jolt he had received when he had picked up the bag the first time. *What the hell?*

He lifted up the satchel and dumped the rest of the contents on the bed. The pictures scattered, leaving a few of them facedown, but two were facing up. A beautiful blond woman with pale eyes was dressed in a simple sheath gown and stood slightly off center, as if there was someone standing next to her just outside of the frame. Nathan poked the corner, and when it didn't shock him, he picked it up. The woman in the image was innocent and childlike, but there was something else about her, something powerful and seductive. He flipped to the next image, but it was nothing but a blur. Nathan reached for the other ones, but they were only shots of canopic jars and some interior shots of the tomb itself—nothing of note. Nathan flipped back through the stack until he was looking at the young woman again. There was something in her eyes, but he couldn't decide whether it was sadness or something else.

Nathan set the stack of photos on the bed and turned his attention back to the camera. He clicked the clamp and watched as the front fell open. He examined it carefully, looking for clues. The lens was intact, the cloth bellows were in working order, and the leather on the outside was barely worn. For all intents and purposes, the camera hadn't aged or changed a bit. It was as if time hadn't touched it in the least. The rack and pinion still moved back and forth to adjust the focus, and the automatic shutter still clicked. The camera was in perfect working order.

But Samuel had two identical cameras. One used film, while the other used glass plates. His father used both mediums, depending on his need. Nathan was unsure of which one this was, but it would be easy enough to identify—not because of the obvious features, but because his favorite camera was engraved with the Eye of Horus. It had been given to his dad as a gift before his first expedition. The eye was considered a sacred symbol, said to protect anything behind it. Samuel would go on and on about its power to keep him safe on his journeys. *A lot of good it did him on his last tour*, Nathan thought.

Nathan flipped over the camera and found what he was searching for. There it was. The "all-seeing eye." Nathan wondered but doubted if there would still be any plates secured in the back. Samuel used to say he preferred to use the plates because of the way they captured the subject, while generally using film for quick shots of artifacts instead. Gingerly, Nathan examined the back and found a plate still in place. As he examined it closer, he noticed something etched onto the glass. He pulled it out and moved it into the light. The girl from the photograph was once again staring back at him—same dress, same look on her face, but instead of the pyramids in the background, there was a halo image behind her.

"That's odd," Nathan said and pulled his glasses out of his suitcase.

He rubbed his fingers over the bright spot to see if it was merely a smudge upon the glass, but it wasn't. Whatever it was, it was imbedded into the glass itself. Upon closer inspection, Nathan noticed a silvery liquid moving under the surface and used his fingernail to try to pry apart the plates to see what it was. The shimmery liquid poured from the slit between the pieces of glass and fell into his hand.

"Mercury?" he whispered.

"Hello?" a woman's voice called out.

Nathan froze. Where had that voice come from? He was alone—or at least, he thought he was. He set the items on the nightstand and walked around the room with the mercury shifting and swirling in his hand. There wasn't anyone here.

"Please don't leave me. I'm here," the voice spoke again.

Nathan was rattled now, and that was saying something, considering all he'd endured when it came to creepy and odd things. He was an Egyptologist, like his father, and had seen countless bizarre and strange occurrences, but this—this was out of the ordinary for sure.

"The glass. Pick it up and look at me."

Nathan took care not to spill the mercury, but he didn't want to continue holding it either. It had long been suspected that its chemical properties caused men to go mad, but he couldn't imagine its effects would happen simply by holding it. Nathan found a small glass vase with a handful of wildflowers on the dresser and decided to pour the mercury into it, but as he started to tip his hand, the voice spoke again.

"No. Hold the liquid and the image," she demanded.

Nathan adjusted his glasses and picked up the glass slide. There on the surface, as clear as could be, was the beautiful young woman he'd seen earlier in the paper photograph. She was smiling a soft smile and holding her hand up in a faint wave.

"Hello," she offered.

"I've lost my damn mind," Nathan replied.

She shook her head. "No, you haven't, but I am so grateful to finally have someone who can see and hear me. Can you free me from this place?"

"Free you? What the hell are you?" Nathan stammered. "I mean, a figment of my imagination, for sure, but how—why?"

"I am trapped here in this prison, and I wish to be free."

CHAPTER 5

"Trapped? Free? What?" Nathan exclaimed in rapid succession as he stared down at the woman talking to him from between the two glass plates. She was *real*, as best as he could tell, and seductive—lord, was she seductive. The thin gossamer-looking gown she wore showed all of her curves along with details he wanted —no needed—to block from his mind, but he was too bewildered not to continue staring at her barely covered skin.

"Please don't be afraid. I do not wish you harm. I only ask to be released."

"Released from what? You have to be a figment of my imagination."

Nathan looked down at his hand and cursed. He was still holding the mercury. That had to be it. He dropped the glass plate onto the bed before hastily grabbing the glass vase. He pulled out the wildflowers, spilling the water out before pouring the mercury into the vessel. *There*, he thought.

He hesitantly glanced at the plate and watched as the female within slammed her fists against the glass. Nathan could see her, but could only faintly hear her cries for help. He eyed his hand and saw a thin residue of the mercury still coating his palm. He rubbed his hand vigorously onto his pant leg, and her voice fell silent. *See, it was the mercury messing with my head.* Nathan picked up the image and saw that she'd dropped to her knees and was sobbing into her hands. *Nope, you're still insane.*

Nathan sat there for a few moments, watching her cry, and began to feel guilty for causing her such pain. He didn't want to see his imaginary dream girl cry. Nathan ran his thumb over her hair and was shocked when she moved. She dried her tears and sat back, looking up at him with the saddest expression he'd ever seen.

"Even if you were real, I don't know what I could do to help you." He watched as her mouth moved, but he couldn't hear anything. "Oh, I understand. The mercury was how I could hear you. Hold on. Let's see." Nathan grabbed the vase and started to faintly hear her again, but it wasn't until he poured the silver substance back into his hand that he heard her voice clearly.

"Please do not be afraid of me. I won't hurt you. I only want out of here. I've been here for so long."

"How long, exactly? Because I cannot wrap my head around the fact that I am sitting in a hotel room, in a town I've never heard of, talking to a beautiful woman trapped in between the plates of a camera lost eighteen years ago."

She stared at him in disbelief. "What did you say?"

"Which part?"

"Eighteen years ago? Where?"

"Egypt. The tomb of Hatshepsut in the Valley of the Kings, to be exact."

Nathan lost sight of the beautiful blonde for a moment.

"Hello? Where did you go?" he called out as he sat up, spilling the mercury in the process. Nathan scrambled to get it back into his hand before she returned to view, but it wasn't working. He continued to chase it, like a spilled egg on a hardwood floor. The mercury was edging close to the Oriental rug, and he needed something to collect it before it soaked into the fibers. Nathan reached for the vase and began scooping its edge against the floor, using his fingers to coax the mercury back inside.

"Where is Samuel?" the woman asked in a rushed tone, her voice faint again.

"Excuse me?" Shocked, Nathan clenched his fist, breaking the vase in his hands. "Shit!" Blood pooled, and the mercury seemed to gravitate toward the cut on his palm. "No!"

Nathan ran out of the room and down the hall to the bathroom to grab a towel and ran back inside, hoping no one had seen him or heard his cursing.

"What's wrong?" he heard her ask when he was back within earshot.

Nathan ignored her as he tried to clean up the broken glass, but she persisted in trying to regain his attention. His hand, however, was bleeding profusely. There was a chunk of glass still embedded in his thumb. Nathan bit his bottom lip and pulled it out. Blood fell in droplets now, and he wrapped the towel around the gash. As he moved to sit on the bed, the glass plate slid off and fell onto the floor, cracking the top piece.

"I can't have this much bad luck." Nathan sighed as he leaned down to pick it up.

The plate had landed right where he'd spilled the mercury, and now the mercury moved, as if deliberately, toward the cracks and crevices. Nathan reached for the plate, but as he did, the edge of the blood-soaked towel he held fell away, and a few drops of blood dripped onto the glass. As soon as it did, Nathan heard a loud pop, and a flame appeared at the plate's center, growing higher and higher. It filled the room until, there before him, stood the beautiful blonde, in the flesh.

CHAPTER 6

*N*athan sat back and stared with his mouth agape as he watched her move. She was real. Living and breathing real. This was not a figment of his imagination, and he was not insane. Good news, he assumed, but still utterly unreal and impossible.

"You freed me?" she said with a hint of disbelief as she took in her corporeal form.

"How? How did I do that?" Nathan stammered. "The mercury was in my hand. My cut. The blood and now, you're real? I must be dreaming."

She spotted the bloody towel and then gazed into Nathan's eyes. "May I?" she asked in a gentle tone.

Nathan was unclear at first as to what she meant, but watched as she reached for the towel. "It's just a cut. I'll be fine."

"I can help," she said, unwrapping the towel.

The blood was no longer gushing, but it was still flowing from the open wound. She touched her finger to the cut, and Nathan watched as gold streaks appeared on her skin. Some were lines, while others were symbols—hieroglyphics, he realized. The symbols pulsed and began to glow, bringing a liquid coursing through her veins and on a path straight to her fingertips, toward his thumb. A moment later, the gold liquid flowed into his cut, healing the wound almost instantly.

"How did you do that?" Nathan asked as he examined his hand.

She met his eyes. "I felt it was the least I could do for your sacrifice in releasing me."

"Yeah, about that." Nathan paused. "I am really confused. I don't know how anything that has happened tonight, or for that matter the events leading up to this past week, are even possible. Who are you? *What* are you? I mean, do you even have a name?" he rambled.

"Yes." She smiled. "My name is Amani."

"I'm Nathan," he replied in a rush.

"I can never thank you enough, Nathan."

"I will take my thank yous with answers, if you don't mind."

"I think you must be related to Samuel," Amani blurted. "I could see him once your blood touched my skin. I could see you as a young boy, though, and not the man you are now."

"You knew my father?" Nathan flinched.

"Samuel is your father?" Amani questioned. "I assumed someone more distant."

"No, Samuel is my father. How do you know him?"

"I don't *really* know him. I met him in Egypt the day my sister and I were planning to leave. That is all. The next thing I knew, I was trapped and alone."

"This doesn't make any sense. And where is your sister now?"

Amani shook her head as tears filled her eyes. "I do not know."

"Maybe my father and your sister are together, then?" Nathan offered, his tone hopeful again.

"Not likely. My sister was not very fond of humans."

"What?" He stood and stepped away from her. "What does that mean? Who are you?"

"I don't think the question is so much who I am, but *what* I am that may concern you."

"No. I am thinking both questions are pertinent here."

Amani sat on the edge of the bed, staring down at her hands. "I believe you were able to free me because your father was the one connected with my entrapment. I've played that day in my mind over and over again, but I come up short for answers every time. Maybe you can help fill in some of the voids."

"Not until you answer why your sister isn't fond of *humans,* as you say. I'm completely confused. If your sister is not human, then what is she? What are you?"

Amani moved to stand, but Nathan backed away, so she sat back down on the edge of the bed. "Please don't be afraid of me."

"I'm not afraid of you," Nathan snapped back.

"But you are. I can sense your fear, and I can hear your thoughts."

"But that is impossible. An improbability."

"I'm surprised, with all you've seen and uncovered, Nathan, that you still question the mystical elements of the world," Amani replied coyly.

He stared at her, but never spoke a word—out loud, that is. *Mystical elements. Like what?* he thought to himself.

Like the Egyptian gods and their purposeful goals of connecting what seems impossible to be connected, she replied in his mind.

Nathan's eyes snapped to his hand, checking for more mercury residue. "How are you doing that?"

"We are connected, your blood to me and my blood to you." She blushed. "We belong to one another now."

"We're *what?*" Nathan shouted.

"Connected," Amani said as she rose and stepped closer to him. Nathan started to move, but calmed the moment her fingers touched his chest. "I don't know how or why I ended up here with you, but I know the gods have their reasons. All I ask is that you give me a chance to explain—to show you we both want the same thing."

"And what is that?" Nathan breathed, uneasy at how close Amani was to him.

"The truth," she whispered.

CHAPTER 7

*a*mani stared at Nathan for a long moment before speaking. "Your eyes are the color of the lotus blooms I remember as a child. Were your mother's eyes blue?"

"Yes," he breathed, his heart racing as she stepped closer.

"And your tawny hair?"

"My father's side."

"You are young."

"I'm old enough to have experienced the world."

Her hand brushed his. "Why does your heart beat so swiftly?"

"Because you are a beautiful woman standing inches from me, and I know in my heart you cannot be real—this whole situation cannot be real."

"I'm here before you. Why do you keep asking if I am real?"

"Because you were in that camera not less than twenty minutes ago."

"You saved me. I am indebted to you."

"What are you, Amani? You're in my thoughts. I can feel you in my blood—my bones." He reached for her, but pulled back. "I feel an electrical current coursing through my body. Why?"

"The connection is possible because I am not like you. I'm otherworldly. Can that not be enough?"

"No. I wish it could be, but ever since I was a boy, I had to know what made things tick. I need to understand everything that has brought me here to this moment. Like how it is possible you are in these photographs," Nathan said, reaching for the pictures on the bed and holding them up for her to see. "And now here before me."

Amani shook her head. "I'm not sure how it is possible," she replied as she held out her hands to look at them. She flipped through each one quickly until she was back at the original image. "Khalida isn't in any of these? It's like she was never there."

"Who is Khalida?"

"My sister," Amani replied shakily.

"Both of you are . . . otherworldly?" Nathan asked as he reached for the photos.

"Yes."

"I was wondering about this one." Nathan pulled out the image of the blur and showed it to Amani. "Any chance, since you are *otherworldly*, you see something more than I do?"

Amani shook her head. "It doesn't look like anything, really," she said hesitantly as she handed him back the photograph. "Can you tell me how Samuel disappeared?"

"The camera and my father disappeared on the same day. No one knows what happened to him exactly, only that he was last seen taking a photograph of two young women—you and your sister, I suppose," he replied and sat back down on the bed. "And then he was gone. What do you know?"

"We met Samuel in the morning, not too long after we were released from our prison. Khalida had seen him with an odd box, and then images of items within the tomb visible on squares of paper. They talked, and he told her it was a camera—that it was used to take pictures of things you'd like to remember, or to document memories. She asked if he would take our photograph."

"And he agreed, obviously."

"Yes. He told us where to stand and not to move, but the flash was bright and startling, then it was over. We weren't certain what would happen next. Khalida wanted to know where the picture was, but he said he needed time to develop them and that he'd have them to us before lunch." Amani sighed. "When we met him again, he said the pictures didn't come out, and he'd like to take new ones. Khalida was angry at needing to do it again, but I convinced her to let him." Tears welled in her eyes. "Then I was trapped, and now I know Samuel went missing too. I'm sorry about your father, Nathan."

"Did he ask you any questions? Wonder why you were wearing what you are wearing? Anything?"

"No," Amani said, looking down at her dress. "Khalida told him our father was one of the men working nearby, and we were just looking at all the astonishing finds—that we were curious about the tombs being opened."

"But that was a lie," Nathan responded.

She nodded her head. "Tombs are sacred spaces and aren't to be disturbed—it is our custom. The fact that we were free was odd and unexpected. We never thought the goddesses would allow it. We were fearful the watchers would find us and trap us again. Khalida made me promise to stay quiet. I had no idea anyone would be hurt as a result. Do you understand?"

"Sort of."

"I can feel your judgment and disappointment, but you have no idea how long it had been since we had seen the real world," Amani added.

Nathan ran his hands through his hair. "It's just that I'd hoped when I found the satchel that it would provide me with clues. Hell, I even hoped when I received the letter from Calla Lily that I'd arrive here in Havenwood Falls and find him alive," Nathan rambled on.

"But instead you found me, and not him," she replied as she moved toward the window. "You said this place is in Colorado, and you received a letter that Samuel's items were here?"

"Yes, and everything about it is as odd as this situation. The last known sighting of this bag was in Egypt. How did it end up here?"

Amani paused before responding. "This place is filled with a magical energy. I can feel it, but I'm unsure of its origin. I cannot sense its source. Maybe magic brought it here."

"Magic? What are you talking about? Is that the explanation for you and the fact that you are *otherworldly*?"

"This Calla Lily you mentioned, may I meet her?" Amani blurted.

"I guess," he stammered, "but it's the middle of the night. I think we'll have to wait until the morning to try to speak with her."

Amani didn't respond. Instead she pulled back the curtain. The street wasn't empty. In fact, it was rather busy for the "middle of the night," as Nathan insisted. There were a few cars on the street and couples milling about, and Amani even saw a wolf heading off toward the woods behind the building across the street. Amani could feel the energy—feel the magic all around her. She laid her hands on the walls and listened to the sounds of the inn.

"What are you doing?" Nathan asked.

Amani remained still, but replied, "Can't you hear it? There are people all around, awake and enjoying life. Someone named Madame Luiza is serving up a plate of meatloaf to a wolf—no, a man—downstairs." Amani turned to Nathan. "What is meatloaf?"

"Wait. You are concerned about meatloaf when you just said there was a wolf man downstairs?"

"Yes," she replied flatly. "He is both man and wolf."

"How do you know this?" Nathan questioned as he reached for her hand. "Amani, please, you have to explain things to me. None of this makes any sense. Perhaps I am actually asleep, and you and all of this have just been a glorious dream."

Amani moved to sit next to Nathan, and when he shifted to the side to make room for her, she paused. "This is not a dream. I am as real as the bed you are sitting on. I told you, I am otherworldly. My kind do not speak of what we are. It draws attention to ourselves and makes the watchers aware. I do not wish to become a person of interest now that I am free. Can you understand that?"

Nathan shook his head slowly. "No, not really."

Amani sat down. "How familiar are you with ancient Egyptian texts?

"Pretty familiar."

"Do you know of the goddess Sekhmet and her brother Shu?" Amani asked.

"Of course."

"I am born of them."

"You are a goddess?"

"No. I am not worthy of such an honor. I am," she paused to find the right words, "I am a daughter of the goddesses Ma'at and Hathor." Amani beamed, pleased with herself.

"Wait, I am confused. I thought you said you were born of Sekhmet and Shu. Ma'at is the goddess of truth and the one all must meet in the Hall of Truth, yes? And Hathor is the goddess of joy and motherhood."

"Yes," she exclaimed, delighted he knew of whom she was speaking. "Khalida and I were both mistakes, but the goddesses Ma'at and Hathor took us under their wings and guided us—kept us safe," she said, her smile suddenly fading. "Sekhmet and Shu are the ones who created us. We are unnatural among our kind."

Nathan reached for her hand. "Okay, but what *kind* is that? Are you an angel or something? I don't know if they have angels in Egyptian mythos, but I think you could fit the bill."

The corner of Amani's mouth curved into a smile as she twirled a lock of Nathan's hair around her finger. "You had curly hair as a boy, too. It was longer then," she replied with a slight tilt of her head. "I think you are much more handsome now."

Nathan blushed and cleared his throat. "You're trying to change the subject."

"Have I upset you with my words?"

"Um, no," he stumbled. "Well, maybe. I'm not used to a woman as stunning as you speaking to me in such a way. The women I know are more," he paused, searching for the right word, "demure, maybe. I don't know. I'm not used to hearing such flattery."

"That is a shame, then. You have a beautiful soul. Any woman would be lucky to have you."

A spark shot between the two of them, but this time, Nathan took the jolt in stride. He knew now it was her. "Why is it sometimes when we touch, there is an electrical charge?"

"I'm sorry." She dropped his lock of hair from her hand. "I do not mean to hurt you. It is part of my curse. I don't like to release it, but I have to let some of it go, so I do it in short bursts. Please forgive me."

"A small price to pay."

"I suppose, but I wish I was different. I wish I was like you."

"I understand you do not want to say how it is we are different, and for now, I will accept that, but I hope that in time, you will trust me enough to tell me the truth. Because I, like you, do not wish to cause you any harm." Amani blushed, and he averted his gaze. "Can you tell me more about Ma'at, Hathor, and your sister?"

She shifted on the bed. "I love and honor the goddesses. They gave me a chance to be more than I was born to be. My hope is when it is time for my soul's heart to be weighed against the feather, that mine will be lighter. It is then the soul can freely be admitted into the Field of Reeds, where I will know nothing but peace and happiness."

"What happens if your heart is not as light as a feather?"

"Should the heart tip the scale, it is thrown to the floor of the Hall of Truth, where it is devoured by Amenti. The soul would cease to exist. This is a fate worse than death."

"I've read texts, but I didn't understand it the same way as you just described it. So this is the Egyptian belief? Does it tie in with why you cannot tell me what you are? Would your truth create an imbalance on the scale?"

Amani shook her head. "No, that is different. By speaking what I am, I put myself in danger, and thus would put you in danger. I won't risk it for either of us."

"Okay," Nathan relented. "Are you tired? Wait, do you even get tired?"

Amani chuckled. "I do, and yes, but not in the same way as you, I assume."

"I figured since we cannot go anywhere, we could rest until the sun is up, and then go to see Calla Lily."

"I would like that." She glanced around and saw nothing but a chair and the bed they were sitting on.

"I can take the chair," Nathan rushed.

"I was going to ask if you minded if I lay here with you. I won't be a bother, but a soft bed does appeal to me."

Nathan quickly gathered the items on the opposite side of the bed and placed them back into the satchel before helping Amani get settled in. He laid a blanket over her before he walked around to lie next to her. He didn't want to appear forward, but her fragrance was intoxicating. She smelled of cinnamon and lavender, and she was still wearing nothing more than a sheer gown that showed almost every inch of her body. She was by far the most beautiful woman he'd ever laid eyes on, and as if that wasn't enough, she was something other than human. For now, Nathan decided, she was his angel—a gift in return for all he'd had to suffer with the loss of his parents. Amani was a new light within his dark world.

CHAPTER 8

The abandoned monastery in Russia Khalida and Khaldun had been hiding in for the past few months had been a perfect refuge after all their wandering. They had traveled the world over, spending months at a time wherever they thought would be suitable. Khalida had never looked back when Khaldun freed her all those years ago. Instead, they reveled in the offerings of the world and made certain not to draw attention to themselves in any way. If the goddesses ever found out, they both knew the punishment would be swift, and they'd never see the light of day again. However, they'd made certain to cover their tracks. There was only one person who could stand in their way, and she would never be revealing their secret.

Khalida stared out the window and watched the sun as it started to make its ascent over the mountains. She hadn't thought about her sister, Amani, in years, and yet something stirred in her—something felt off.

"She's been released. Someone has found the camera and set her free," Khalida raged.

"I've heard nothing. Not even a whimper. How can you be sure?"

"I'm sure. Why would I be telling you if it wasn't so?"

"Calm down. I will track her, and I will end her."

"You cannot kill her, you fool. If she dies, I die, remember?"

Khaldun moved closer to Khalida. "I've forgotten nothing," he said as he loomed over her. "I will take care of the situation."

Khalida glared at him. "You'll need my help to do it. She is smart and will not call out our kind to draw the watchers. I can sense her only because of our bond."

"Then where is she?"

Khalida closed her eyes and did her best to sense Amani. She assumed Amani was shadowing herself, because the link between them felt like the flicker of a candle being blown by the wind—glowing but not steadily. "I'm not certain. She is not close, and it is someplace obscure and hidden from view."

"I'll need more to go on than that," Khaldun chided.

"You may be my savior, but you are not my master," she pushed back. "That is all I can see. The rest is nothing more than a view from a window. She could be anywhere," Khalida said, stepping away from him.

Khaldun grabbed her wrist and shoved her against the wall with her arms above her head.

"I love it when you are irate," he said as he pressed himself against her, tilting his head downward to taste her lips.

She smirked as his lips grew nearer. "I don't get irate these days. Nothing much to fret over, with you around."

"Well then, let me properly piss you off so I can have you the way I prefer you, my love," he said, tightening his grip around her wrists.

As he claimed her mouth, she moaned at his forcefulness and retaliated by biting his bottom lip, drawing blood. Khaldun laughed and ran his heavily tattooed hand up her torso, cupping her breast, tightening his grip. "I do not remember what my life was like before you, and I will die before I ever have to do without you."

Khalida ran her tongue over the blood pooling on his lips, and the silver symbols on her skin began to shimmer. Khaldun pulled the tie on the dressing gown she wore and let it fall to the floor. Her raven hair was a sharp contrast to her pale skin. All of her was exposed, and he groaned when she pressed up against him.

"I think you need to show me how much you love me and the

lengths you are willing to go to keep the truth of me being alive hidden," she said against his lips. "Because if the goddesses find out I'm free, and have been for eighteen years, we will both be punished, if not killed."

Khaldun let his fingers dive into her sweet heat and assaulted her mouth with his tongue. He needed to claim her. No, they needed to claim each other before their djinn natures, then their budding passion would simmer, and they'd return to their human façades. Khaldun's true nature had been released, and nothing but sex or violence would settle the vibrant blue glow writhing within the lines of his tattoos. Khalida was the same, only her tattoos were not tattoos at all. They were hieroglyphs etched into her skin that shimmered silver, depending upon her mood.

She'd been forced all her life to hide who and what she was. The goddesses expected her to be more like her holier-than-thou sister, but ever since she'd been with Khaldun, she could be all she was, without fear of him shunning her for it. They were quite the pair, a watcher and the watched, in love and in hiding. Nothing else mattered but being together. They'd risked everything the day she and Amani were released. It had been a mistake or fate, depending on how you viewed it, but nonetheless, the outcome was exactly as it should be.

Khalida had met Khaldun when she and Amani were originally imprisoned. He was a watcher of wayward djinn—djinn who'd fallen out of favor with the gods and goddesses. Shortly after the twins were captured, Khaldun was assigned the duty of reporting any incidents that gave him pause—anything that could endanger the world if they were ever to be released.

The twin girls were unique and more powerful than expected. Their power was too great and thus was supposed to have been hidden away forever. No one could have predicted human archaeologists would unearth them and inadvertently release them. It was a misfortune Khalida and Khaldun took full advantage of.

Khalida didn't dwell on the day she was freed. She'd made certain she'd remain alive, but without Amani to keep her from living her life as she saw fit. However, now that she could sense her sister, things would have to change once again.

"Your mind is elsewhere, and I need your sole focus," Khaldun commanded as he moved his fingers purposely to bring her attention back to the present.

Khalida arched her back and moaned. "I'm focused."

"You are now," he said, hovering over her naked body.

Khaldun waited until she was ready for release before he entered her. The two writhed in pleasure until they both were sated. The moment they came, the symbols on their skin ceased to pulse. Their djinn sides were satisfied, and now they could focus on what lay before them.

Khalida sighed, and Khaldun pulled her closer. "I will find Amani, and I will fix this for us. Nothing has changed."

"I want to believe that, but I've evaded my fate for too long. I'm afraid now something drastic will have to happen to make any of this right, and we still haven't found a way to unlink my and Amani's lifelines."

"We don't need to. We will simply trap her again, and this time, we'll make sure she'll never be found," he said, and kissed her. "We'll make a plan tomorrow. For now, sleep."

Khalida was strong, hardened to the world, but in Khaldun's arms, she was a young girl in love with a man twice her age and three times her strength. Just as he was putty in her hands. She knew he'd go to the ends of the earth for her, and soon they were about to find out how far that journey would take them both.

CHAPTER 9

$\mathcal{N}$athan woke to the sound of Amani moaning and writhing on the bed. At first he thought something was wrong, but as he watched her, he realized she appeared as though she was pleasuring herself. He was shocked. Never before had he seen a woman like this. Nathan knew he should try to wake her, but he too was aroused as he watched her move her hands over her now exposed breasts. He wondered what she could be dreaming about that would have her doing what she was doing. However, when she called out the name Khaldun, he wondered who that could be. A lost love, perhaps?

Nathan moved to sit up and froze when he heard her gasp and cry out. Amani looked over at him, his hands in the air in hopes she'd understand it wasn't him touching her. She blushed and fixed her dress to cover herself.

"I—I don't understand. What was happening to me?"

Nathan shook his head. "I—I don't know," he replied in a rush. "I woke up, and you were—um, well, yeah."

Amani sat up and bowed her head. "I've never felt my sister's emotions so vividly and so . . ." She trailed off.

Nathan stood, grabbed the blanket that had fallen on the floor, and wrapped it around her shoulders before stepping away. "It seemed like you were dreaming or in a trance. You said the name Khaldun. Do you know who that is?"

Amani's eyes went wide, and she stared at Nathan, as though unsure of what to say.

"Is he your betrothed or something? Husband?"

"No," Amani snapped. "I am not mated. I've never been with a man in such a way."

"Oh, well, who is this Khaldun, then?"

"He is a watcher. Our guardian. Assigned to watch over Khalida and me. Nothing more."

"Okay, well, what do you think it meant that you were . . . um . . . ," Nathan stammered, "calling out his name?"

"There is only one way." Rage fell over Amani's features. "I was feeling my sister's emotions. She is alive and doing well, it seems."

"You two are *that* connected? Wow."

"We are twins. Forced to feel one another's emotions. Our lifelines are interconnected. If one of us dies, the other will follow. The same is true with everything else."

"Are you kidding?"

She shook her head. "No. I have not been able to sense her all this time. I assume it's because I was trapped in your father's camera, but now that I am free, our link will reconnect, and she will be able to sense me, too."

"Is that bad?"

"I don't know, exactly. I guess it will depend on if my sister is *with* Khaldun, or if she is his captive."

Nathan crossed to the window and opened the curtains. "It's morning. We can go talk to Calla Lily and see if she has any information about how the camera came to be in her possession."

Amani nodded and pulled the blanket around her tighter. "It's a start, at least."

Nathan checked his watch. It was barely seven o'clock, but when he opened the door to the hall, the smell of breakfast cooking tempted his every sense.

"Are you hungry?" Nathan said as he opened the door to their room. "They're serving breakfast downstairs. We can grab something to eat before going to see Calla Lily, if you're interested."

"Will they be serving the meatloaf you spoke of?"

Nathan laughed. "We do not eat meatloaf for breakfast."

"Then what do you eat? Grains and beer?"

"No, we eat eggs, bacon, toast, and potatoes."

"Okay," Amani said as she stood, the blanket slipping off her shoulders as she did. Nathan sucked in a breath, and Amani looked down at her dress. "What's wrong?"

"I think you should wear this," he replied as he reached for his coat and offered it to Amani. "At least until we can get you something *more* to wear."

"I don't understand. What is wrong with what I am wearing?"

Nathan paused to gather his words so as not to offend her. "Women of the day tend to wear more modest clothing. I'm not sure the people of Havenwood Falls will understand why you're not covered."

"Oh," Amani breathed.

Nathan held out the frock coat for her to put on, and she took it without another word. He buttoned the front and stared at her for a moment.

"You look great both ways," Nathan said, before he kissed her forehead and reached for her hand. "Besides, if I'm being honest, I don't want any other man looking at you the way I look at you."

Amani blushed and squeezed his hand.

The two walked down the hall and took the stairs to head toward the dining room. Madame Luiza grinned when she saw Nathan.

"Only here a day, and you've already found a beautiful young woman to accompany you to breakfast?" She cast a glance at Amani. "You're lovely."

"What are you?" Amani asked.

"That's an odd question, dear."

"Not really. You are something different, but nothing I've encountered."

"What can I get you two for breakfast?" Madame Luiza said with an emotionless smile.

"Two of whatever you are serving sounds great," Nathan blurted, hoping to ease the awkwardness.

"I'll get right on it. You can sit right over there, Nathan."

"Thank you, Madame Luiza. She's not familiar with the social mores of the time. I'm sorry. I don't think she meant any offense."

She patted him on the shoulder. "None taken. We'll get you fed and then you can take a walk around the town," Madame Luiza said before stopping short. Amani was walking toward the table, and Madame Luiza's eyes went to her feet. "Where are her shoes?"

Nathan's eyes went wide. *Shoes. How could I have forgotten shoes for her?*

"She must have forgotten them upstairs. I'll make sure to grab her a pair before we head out," Nathan said in a rush.

"Very well. I'll bring your food to the table here soon."

"Thank you."

Nathan looked at his watch as Amani was taking her last bite of toast. It was eight o'clock, and he was anxious to see Calla Lily—anxious to see if she could explain where she got the camera from. Maybe then he could understand who and what Amani was.

"Are you ready to go?"

"Yes," Amani replied after she swallowed her toast.

"Was everything to your liking?" Madame Luiza asked as she reached for their empty plates.

"Your food is wonderful. Almost magical, in fact," Amani replied. "I've never had toast before. Especially with this wiggly blue stuff."

"It's blueberry jam." Madame Luiza laughed. "It's homemade."

"I like it very much."

"Well, I will save you some for tomorrow."

Nathan stood and pulled out the chair for Amani. "Your cooking is delicious," he added.

"I'll expect you both for dinner later."

"We'll be here." Nathan grinned. "I was wondering how I get to Calla Lily's shop."

"That's easy. Out the front door and to the left. Go down Main Street, and it'll be on your left. She opens promptly at eight-thirty, and if I know her, she'll be expecting you."

"Normally, I would say that was odd, but after the past twenty-four hours, nothing is shocking. I will welcome her foresight."

When they walked out of the dining hall, Nathan asked Amani to stay put. "We don't have any shoes for you to wear, so I am going to grab a pair of mine until we can get you ones of your own. Okay?"

She nodded and watched him as he took the steps two at a time. Nathan returned a few moments later with a pair of work boots.

"Here, put these on," he said, kneeling down to help her into them. "They'll keep your feet warm too."

When he stood back up, they were face to face with one another. Amani reached up and touched his face. "You are so kind to me."

"It's nothing," he said offhandedly. "Ready to go?"

Amani nodded as Nathan reached for her hand.

The two of them walked slowly over the cobblestone streets, Amani tripping slightly in the boots that were at least four sizes too big for her.

"Can you smell the dew on the spruce trees or hear the heartbeat of the Aspens?" she asked distractedly, her head tipped toward the sky.

Nathan looked at her. "No. How can you?"

"I'm connected to the energy of all nature," she said as they reached the storefront, "and this place pulses with it."

CHAPTER 10

*I*t was 8:23 on the dot when Nathan and Amani arrived at Callie's Trinkets and What Nots, and as Madame Luiza had said, she was waiting for them.

"I trust you enjoyed your breakfast," Calla Lily said as she opened the door.

Nathan simply shook his head. "What is it with this town? You and Madame Luiza seem to just *know* things."

"I told you, Nathan. It's filled with a magical energy. Everyone here has a gift," Amani replied, matter-of-factly.

"Something like that," Calla Lily said, motioning for Amani and Nathan to come in. "Welcome to Havenwood Falls . . ." Her voice trailed off for a second before continuing, "I'm sorry, I don't know your name."

"Amani," she replied as she stepped inside.

Calla Lily tilted her head to Nathan as he stepped in behind Amani. "Your name means wishes and desires. How apropos."

Amani turned back to Calla Lily. "You are very gifted. Most do not know that."

Nathan watched the two women for a moment before shifting his focus to the store.

"Your shop is quite large and well stocked with treasures," he remarked, eyeing a glass chalice with a Greco-Roman scene featured on the front of it. "Is this a . . . ?"

"It is."

"And are these . . . ?"

"They are."

"How did you come to acquire such treasures?" The excitement in Nathan's voice was unmistakable.

"Sometimes in the same way I acquired your father's satchel."

Nathan arched his brow. "And how was that exactly?"

"Unexpectedly," she replied.

Amani, too, was mesmerized by the large space. It was filled with this and that—treasures or trash, depending on who was looking. To Amani, everything was beautiful, new, and interesting. She wandered over to a rack of clothes near the window and ran her hands over them. The unique fabrics, textures, and colors were all so different from what she was used to. She'd worn nothing but a sheer linen sheath for centuries. "These are beautiful."

"You're more than welcome to try on anything you like," Calla Lily said as she looked over at Nathan. "Your boots and coat, I presume?"

He sighed and crossed his arms in front of his chest. "Yes. She is in need of some clothes in the same way I am in need of some answers."

Calla Lily grinned. "How about we start with her first, and then we can move on to the questions and answers."

Nathan nodded and laughed as he watched Amani twirl with a dress in her hand. "That's probably a good idea."

Amani and Calla Lily worked together to gather some clothes and shoes to try on. When they'd narrowed it down to a few things, Nathan interjected his opinion. It didn't take long for Amani to find an outfit she looked amazing in, but then again, he was sure she'd look good in a potato sack. Nathan couldn't take his eyes off Amani. He watched Calla Lily fix her hair and wondered what it was about her that had him so enthralled. None of this made any sense, but even if he was willing to indulge the fantasy, what would the future look like for him, for her—for them? She wasn't human, and he was. How was that going to work? Perhaps Calla Lily's information about his father's satchel would come with answers about Amani and whether or not she could remain with him, but for now, he'd simply enjoy the moment.

"How do I look?" Amani asked.

Nathan stared at her for a long moment before replying, "Beautiful. It seems to be my favorite word to describe you."

Amani's smile radiated. "Oh, good. I was hoping it would please you. I couldn't tell what you were feeling when you were watching me try on all those garments."

Nathan took her hand in his. "It was joy. Nothing more."

Amani's smile faded. "Why are you lying?"

"I'm not lying . . . exactly," Nathan replied as he dropped his head. "I'm trying to understand all of this and thinking about how we go forward from here is all."

Amani reached up and placed her hand over his heart. "One step at a time until we find the answers we seek."

He exhaled a breath and put his hand on hers. "One step at a time then."

They both turned to see Calla Lily watching them from behind the counter. "How about we start with one answer at a time," she offered.

Nathan took Amani's hand, and the two of them walked over to Calla Lily. "We are going to be here a while. We have lots of questions."

"I've got all day." She grinned. "What shall we start with? I promise nothing but honesty."

"What are you?" Amani asked. "I know you are something, but I've never encountered anyone like you. You are otherworldly, like me, are you not?"

"I'm sorry. She keeps asking everyone that," Nathan replied nervously.

"It's fine, and she's right. I'm what's referred to as a gypsy," she said, and turned to show them the mark of the gypsies on the back of her neck. "I have the ability to *read* you," Calla Lily admitted.

"You're a mystic?" Nathan blurted. "I mean, not that there is anything wrong with that," he offered, realizing he may have unintentionally offended her.

"No offense taken, Nathan, and yes, I am, but I am more than a mystic."

"Do you know, then, what I am?" Amani asked.

"I have an idea, but I've never encountered your kind either. I can see more if you let me," she said, reaching for Amani's hand. "I can tell a lot by your palm, and I can tell you even more if I use my tarot cards."

"Can you fill in the missing pieces for us? We are lost. We do not understand how it is that I came to be here. I was in Egypt with my sister, Khalida, and I knew Samuel, well, met him," she corrected, "before I lost my sister and was trapped."

"And it seems like my father's disappearance is connected to Amani's entrapment."

"I'll do my best," Calla Lily said as Amani turned her hand over so her palm was visible. "You said you were with your sister?"

"Yes, but she was lost to me. I thought she had died, but now that I am out of the camera, I can sense her, but I cannot pinpoint where she is exactly."

"Havenwood Falls is a special place. The disconnect between you and Khalida may be due to the magic surrounding us."

"What?" Nathan questioned.

"Why are you shocked, Nathan?" Calla Lily laughed. "You had to have some clue. It's part of the reason you are here to begin with."

He rubbed his forehead. "Nope. Completely clueless. Just hoping I'd encounter a miracle."

She cast a glance at Amani. "In a way, you did."

Nathan blew out a burst of air and ran his fingers through his hair. "I guess you're right."

"Khalida is more than your sister—she's your twin. It is a bond stronger than siblings," Calla Lily said as she continued to examine the lines on Amani's hand. "Your parents were human, but they are not your blood. You are something different."

Amani nodded as she held her breath. "Yes."

"What are you, Amani?" Calla Lily asked skeptically, running her hands along the fate line.

"She can't tell you," Nathan interjected. "That is why we are here. I'd hoped *you* could tell me, because she can't. Amani is forbidden to speak it, or it will draw the watchers' attention, and that is not good, apparently."

Calla Lily released Amani's hand. "Hmm. Okay."

"Why hmm? What's wrong?" Nathan asked.

"I do not know what these symbols mean that are interlaced with the lines. I've never seen them before. I mean, they look like hieroglyphics, but I can't be sure."

"They are," Amani replied.

"May I see?" Nathan asked.

She gave Nathan her hand. "Hmm. Well this one is the symbol for life, and this one is the symbol for protection. Here," he pointed, "is the symbol for the Ka, and this one here is a feather, which could represent a few things."

"It is for the goddess Ma'at," Amani said, then pointed to the next hieroglyph. "And this is for Hathor, and this one here is . . ."

"The Eye of Horus," Nathan interrupted. "The all-seeing eye."

Amani nodded.

"Why would these be interlaced with your lifeline, Amani?" Calla Lily asked.

"I'm not certain." She shrugged. "I told you, I'm unique . . . Khalida and I both are."

Calla Lily sank back in her chair, disappointment furrowing her brow as she strained to look deeper. Unfortunately, within seconds, she released Amani's hand and confessed, "I'm not sure I can help. I see a lot, but with you, I am blocked from seeing your past or your future. It's all a hazy mess."

CHAPTER 11

"The tarot cards you spoke of. Can they show the past?"

"They can," Calla Lily replied and drew out her deck to set them on the counter. "They can tell the present and the future, too, but you have to understand how they work. Have you ever used this type of divination?"

Amani shook her head.

Calla Lily began to shuffle the deck, but Amani put her hands over them. "May I connect to you to understand them?"

Calla Lily gave her a quizzical look. "Of course."

Amani closed her eyes and used her power to see into Calla Lily's thoughts. She didn't want to pry into anything personal. She only wanted to understand enough to show Nathan and Calla Lily what she was unable to speak.

A few moments passed, and the cards began to fly one by one in a line from the table up into the air. In the open space at the center of the shop, the tarot deck swirled like a roaring tornado for a few moments before landing on the floor in a perfect Celtic Cross Spread.

Calla Lily was in awe. "You're a fast learner," she said as she walked over toward the cards.

Amani opened her eyes and smiled. "I promise I only looked into what I needed. Nothing more."

"I know. I could sense where you were in my mind."

"I have no idea what is going on," Nathan interjected, "but as long as you two do, that's all that really matters."

Calla Lily lifted the hem of her skirt and knelt down to get a closer look at the spread. The first card and the card related to Amani was the World. It was reversed with the Justice card lying across it. She looked over her shoulder at Amani. "You certainly know how to make things clear, now don't you?"

"I will need you both to brace yourself for what is to come when you get to the Temperance card. There is only one way for me to tell you without actually speaking it," Amani said as she wrung her hands together. "Before my mother died, I saw her memories. I've never told anyone this, not even Khalida," she said before swallowing hard. "I always feared the judgment if anyone knew the truth. I loved my mother and father and never wanted any harm to come to them."

Nathan was a little peaked, but he was also nodding his head in agreement.

"Okay then, what do you want me to do?" Calla Lily asked.

Amani closed her eyes. "Pick up the card."

Calla Lily glanced at the grounding card. It was the Tower. The card associated with shocking change and catastrophe. Mix that with the Temperance card in the reversed position, and this was going to be a journey. Calla Lily reached up for Nathan's hand. "I'm not sure what is going to happen, so please hold on."

Nathan gave her a quick, false smile and took hold of her hand.

The moment Calla Lily touched the card, the room began to spin. Suddenly, they were no longer in Callie's Trinkets and What Nots, but instead were in an unfamiliar place, watching as events played out before them like a motion picture.

Neema knew it was odd to check in on adult children as they slept, but the day she had dreaded for twenty-five years was finally here. Where had the time gone? They were just babes in her arms, and now they were grown

women. *Beyond their prime, some would say, for marrying and having children of their own, but Neema and her husband had not pushed the girls toward marriage. Instead, they tutored them in multiple languages and various cultures, broadening their scope of knowledge. They were as smart as any man and as cunning as the pharaoh's own children. It had been a choice on their part to make them of supreme value. Neema even hoped maybe they could rule one day, if given the chance.*

As Neema watched Amani and Khalida sleep, she was anxious to see what, if anything, would change. Would they even change at all? Would it happen when the moon was at its peak in the night sky? Maybe the prophecy had been false; maybe having her as a mother changed their fates. Neema thought back to the day when her world shifted. She wasn't the one who'd given them life, because she and her husband were both human. She was, though, the one who loved and cared for them every day and every moment. They were her treasures, yet as the days quickened toward their maturity, she began to fear the truth of who they really were.

Amani and Khalida were djinn, or so she was told, but to her, they were precious angels in need of love and care. She was warned to watch for any signs of peculiarity, because djinn could be tricksters, but the girls had never been anything other than sweet and kind. Every djinn aged a quarter of a century before their powers and talents were revealed. However, Amani and Khalida were not typical djinn. They were something else—something unique—and that was the reason they lived among the humans and not their own kind. Neema liked to believe their uniqueness was meant to save the world one day or to heal the sick.

The corner of her mouth quirked up as she looked down at her girls. Amani slept soundly, but Khalida was tossing and turning—nothing out of the ordinary. Satisfied they were okay, Neema decided to pray to Hathor and Ma'at for guidance instead of worrying the entire night away.

Neema plucked a single feather from a dove and placed it into a pile of burning embers. As the feather began to burn, she lifted the copper dagger from the altar she'd prepared and pricked her finger, letting the blood pool before swirling with her offerings. Neema removed the ankh from the cord around her neck and placed it over the ashes of the feather. She patiently waited for Hathor to appear. When nothing happened, Neema sighed.

Maybe it was a sign. She walked over to the chair on the open balcony and sat down stiffly, awaiting the goddesses' return. As she stared into the distance, a gentle wind caressed her skin, lulling Neema to sleep. Her thoughts drifted to the day the twins were born.

On the day of their birth, Neema gave Amani and Khalida names to enhance their souls, as was her belief. The soul was made up of five parts—the Jb: the heart; the Sheut: the shadow; the Ren: the name; the Ba: the personality; and the Ka: the soul—and it was Neema's plan to ensure they'd be worthy on the day they'd meet the goddess Ma'at by bestowing them with names to suit who they were as part of the universe. Neema honored all Egyptian traditions, and had since she was a young girl. Especially anything honoring Hathor and Ma'at.

Neema had been born of privilege and was married to a man of wealth and prestige, but she had a secret only she and the goddess Hathor knew. Neema had been unable to produce an heir, and her husband was growing weary of her infertility. She prayed night and day for Hathor to bless her with a child, and finally the goddess appeared before her with a proposal—one she would not refuse.

"I've heard your prayers, child, and I've come to give you what you ask," Hathor said in a gentle tone.

"I will do anything," Neema begged, "please."

"Twin girls were born of fire and air, but not human girls. These djinn will require watching over—careful watching. Do you believe you are worthy of the task?"

Neema dropped to her knees and looked up at the powerful deity. "I do. I only want my belly to swell and to feel the link of mother and child. Will they know I am theirs, as they are mine?"

"They will only know you as their mother, but you may never tell anyone of this night. Only you are to know, understand?"

"Yes, goddess. I will love them as my own."

"On the twenty-fifth year of their birth, you are to make a sacrifice in my name and burn it, letting the smoke rise and billow. When the flames recede, you are to place this ankh into the ashes, and I will come to you once again," Hathor said, handing Neema the golden symbol of life.

Neema bowed and held the ankh to her chest.

"Go now to your husband and seduce him. Make certain he is fully pleasured, and when you wake, the twins will be within your womb."

Tears spilled down Neema's cheeks. *"Thank you, Goddess. Thank you for these gifts."*

"I do hope by giving you these girls that they will turn into worthy beings."

"I will make it so. I will be a good mother."

"Be well, Neema. I will return to you when they come of age," Hathor said solemnly before disappearing from view.

Neema rose, fixing her hair and gown before going to do as the goddess asked. Her husband had been sleeping, but could easily be roused by Neema's touch. Tonight her belly would fill with not just one, but two children, and it pleased Neema to not only show her husband, Garai, how much she loved him, but also how virile he was to produce twins. Their children would not be male heirs, but they would still be a blessing. Neema caressed her husband until she had his attention and then let the thin wisp of material fall from her shoulders onto the floor, exposing her bare flesh and rousing every bit of Garai's senses.

The couple made love for hours, the moon's glow illuminating Neema's tawny skin as she writhed above her husband. They both seemed engulfed by the flames of desire. It was as if they'd never tasted one another, and this was their first moment of ecstasy. Neither wanted it to end.

As the sun began to rise, the couple lay in each other's arms, sated and exhausted. The slaves entered to bring them trays of fruit and beer, but noticed their sleeping masters and quietly left the room. Garai and Neema spent the day in bed, not bothering to rise until the sun began to set. Garai seemed pleased with himself, often commenting that their escapades of the previous night were sure to produce the child they so desperately sought. Neema contentedly ran her hands over her womb, knowing he'd be pleased with Hathor's gifts as much as she was.

Neema grabbed a handful of grapes and a few figs before striding back over to Garai. As he watched her walk to him, her breasts appeared fuller, and the gentle curve of her hips seemed to fill out with each step she took. His chest filled with pride in knowing his seed had taken hold. Neema's naked body was luxurious, and he wanted to taste her once again. When she reached his side, he pulled her into his arms and rolled her onto the bed. Neema giggled and fed him a fig.

"What has you so boyish, my love?"

Garai licked his lips and ran his hands over Neema's swelling belly. "This. You. Our soon-to-be family."

"But how can you be so sure?" she teased.

"You already have the glow of a woman bearing a child," he said and kissed her.

Neema grinned inwardly. "Then I shall praise Hathor for her gift and honor her in every way."

Garai grinned and let his hands roam until he could no longer control his desire. He entered her, and the waves of passion once again ignited between them.

Neema was jolted from the memory of her and Garai when the sound of footfalls resonated behind her.

"Mother!" Amani cried out. "Come quickly. Something is wrong with Khalida."

Neema jumped to her feet and ran with Amani to Khalida's side.

"What is wrong with her, Mother? Why is her hair alternating between dark and white?" Amani asked.

"I do not know." Neema's voice quivered as she watched gold symbols appear and disappear on Amani's back as well.

Khalida's eyes opened, and she stared blankly at her mother and sister. Neema gasped, and Amani cried out as they watched Khalida's eyes change from a golden amber to an opaque white, then back to amber.

"Oh, Sister. What has happened to you?" Amani pleaded.

Khalida reeled back and asked the same, as fissures of fire erupted over Amani's caramel-colored skin. Symbols took shape and etched words in ancient script over her entire body. Amani dropped to her knees and begged her mother for answers.

Tears welled in Neema's eyes. "I'm sorry. I should have told you long ago, but it was forbidden. I'm so sorry, my precious girls. Your Ren means wishes and aspirations, just as Khalida's means immortal. You two are my immortal wishes, and I love you both."

Neema ran to the altar and pleaded to Hathor to appear immediately, *but nothing happened. Maybe the sacrifice was not great enough. She gripped the dagger in her hand and plunged it into her chest. "I beg of you, Hathor, protect my girls as I have protected your secret," Neema cried out. "I sacrifice myself to save them."*

Amani ran to her side and held her dying mother in her arms. "Mother, no! Why would you do this? We need you."

Neema brushed back a golden lock from Amani's face. "You've been my greatest gift. Forgive me. All I did was for love—always love."

Khalida strode over to Neema. "What secrets?" she asked coolly.

Tears spilled from Neema's eyes as her blood pooled around her. Khalida had always been the mischievous one of the two. She always searched for trouble, while Amani kept the peace. As Neema looked at them now, their djinn sides revealing themselves, it became clear. Amani with her dark, dusky grey skin and flaming hair, and Khalida with her pure white hair and fawn skin. They were light and dark, merged as one yet split in two."

When the day comes for your souls to be weighed, make certain your heart is worthy," Neema whispered.

Khalida's eyes narrowed as she look at Neema. "Are you even our mother?"

Amani gasped. "You dare ask such a question!"

"Always the naïve one, sister. Look at us. Do we look like her?"

Amani looked down at her changed skin and then up at her sister's now white hair, still refusing to acknowledge the truth. Neema squeezed Amani's hand, shifting her attention back to her mother.

"I am your mother in all the ways that make a mother. I carried you in my womb. I gave birth to you and suckled you at my breast. I cared for you every day. Loved you like no other, but you are not of my blood. You are so much more than blood and bone. Be true and remember my peace and joy, and always my love," Neema said, the last three words in barely a whisper, before dying in Amani's arms.

Tears spilled from Amani's eyes, while Khalida stood defiant.

"Our life is built on lies," Khalida hissed.

"She may have lied, but she did love us. She was, as she said, our

mother in all the ways that mattered." Amani cried as she stared down at her blood stained hands.

Just then the door slammed open, and Garai stormed in.

"What is all the ruckus?" he demanded. As he continued into the room, he saw a stranger holding his wife's lifeless body and flew into a rage.

Amani looked up at him with her now darkened skin and realized he didn't recognize her.

"What have you done?" he cried out as he tore Neema from her arms.

"We've done nothing. Neema did this to herself," Khalida spat.

"Neema? Never. Who are you to say such words?" Garai growled.

"Khalida means no disrespect, Father," Amani interjected.

"Father? I am not your father. Guards!"

"Do not call him Father. He is no more our father than she was our mother."

Garai narrowed his eyes at the two strangers before him.

Amani slowed her breathing and wished the changes that turned them into this would stop and he could see them as they truly were. Even as she thought it, her skin flickered and her hair fell in golden waves over her shoulders. "See father, it is us, your daughters."

"What are you?" Garai asked in confusion as he watched her change into the daughter he knew. He shook his head, whispering to Neema as he rocked her. "What have you done, my love? What have our daughters become? Demons? Sorcerers? Witches?"

"I'm sorry, father," Amani pleaded.

"Your mother gave everything to you, and this is the way you repay her—with lies?"

"Lies?" Khalida said as she moved to strike Garai.

Amani pleaded with her sister to back off and walk away, but when Khalida refused, Amani blocked Neema and Garai from her view.

"What is wrong with you?" Amani shouted.

"Different, it seems. We are powerful. Can you not feel it coursing through your veins? I want to see what we can do, don't you?" Khalida replied with a sinister grin, the djinn traits once again surfacing.

"You will never hurt them, Sister—never!"

"Neema is already gone. He is all who remains, and he never did anything but force his will upon us. We are free now."

Amani's heart began to break as the truth began to settle in for her father. His beloved wife was now dead, and the truth that his daughters were not really his was sinking in. Lies begat more lies even as Amani tried to defend him and Neema against Khalida.

"I have loved both you both equally, but Khalida, you have always challenged my authority. I know it must have come across as me treating you differently, but even in harsh tones, you had my heart and my love, Khalida. You both did," he cried.

Neema was gone, but he needed answers, so he pleaded for the goddess that Neema held so dear to show herself.

"Hathor, I demand to know the truth."

No one answered.

"Please, dear goddess. I must know why my beloved is dead and my daughters are not as they once were. I beg of you."

Amani and Khalida's argument stopped in an instant when the curtains began to whip near the balcony's edge. Smokeless fire and the scent of frankincense rose until it was pungent in the air. Three figures appeared before them, unseen until the fire cleared. They stepped forward, and Garai and Amani gasped as a larger-than-life guard with ebony skin and the face of a jackal stood holding a canopic jar, glaring down at the twin girls. Next to him was a frightening male, dressed all in black, his skin etched like Khalida's and Amani's, but glowing a vibrant cobalt blue. He, too, stared at them, his arms crossed loosely in front of his chest as if he were at ease, but nothing about his demeanor expressed calm. He appeared as if he could rip them limb from limb in a matter of seconds.

In the middle towered a beautiful woman dressed in ceremonial garb and adorned with jewels and headdress befitting a queen. Amani was the first to realize who she was and immediately dropped to her knees and bowed her head. Khalida stood defiant, and when Garai looked from his daughters to the goddess, he too bowed his head.

"You will not honor me?" Hathor asked Khalida.

"I know not who you are, but can assume you have something to do with the lies that have been told here."

59

Hathor tilted her head in curiosity. "I believe you do know who I am, but still refuse. You will, however, pay me the respect I deserve." Hathor's eyes changed, and she stepped toward Khalida. "BOW!" she commanded.

Khalida unwillingly took to her knees.

"I am sick of your childish games," Hathor said as she hovered above her.

Khalida stared at her through opaque eyes. "I'm not playing games. I'm tired of being lied to."

Amani scolded Khalida under her breath, pleading with her to stop before the goddess killed them all.

Once Hathor was satisfied, she went over to where Garai knelt, Neema's lifeless body still in his arms. "May I see her?" she asked reverently.

Garai shifted so he could give Hathor access to Neema. "Why did she do this? Why are Amani and Khalida something otherworldly?" Garai questioned, the words catching on the lump in his throat.

Hathor brushed the hair back from Neema's face. "It is time for her to walk with Anubis. I know she will pass Ma'at's test and enter the afterlife without negative judgment. I will make certain Ma'at knows of Neema's love and good deeds."

"But she lied," he replied.

"A lie she was bound to by her commitment to me. She wanted to bear your children, but was unable. I gave her the twins as a gift—with one condition. She was to never reveal this to anyone, not even you, Garai. She honored her word and loved you and the girls as I expected her to."

"So why did she take her own life?"

"Sacrifice. She knew there would be one. This was never my intent, but no one knew what the twins would turn out to be—that is, until now."

"Will you take them from me?" Garai asked.

"I will have to."

"Then I ask only one thing of you. If you are to take my beloved daughters as you have taken Neema, then I wish to walk beside her in the Duat. Grant me this, please. I do not want to live a life without her."

Hathor bowed her head in acknowledgment, and the frightening male with the tattooed skin stepped forward, his markings calming from to cobalt to black. Amani cried as she stared at her father. There were no words spoken, no time before the man jammed a dagger into Garai's side. Garai's body slumped to the ground, and Amani was shaken. She knew she risked punishment, but she would hold her father as she held her mother in those final moments.

Amani cradled his head in her lap as he spoke his final words. "I love you, Amani. You and Khalida may not be of my blood, but you are of my heart."

"I love you, Father. Please be well until we can be together once more," Amani said as she slipped the ring and jewel-encrusted bracelet off her arm and placed them into his hands. "An offering, in case you should need it."

Garai squeezed Amani's hand and took one last breath. She swallowed hard and did her best to steady herself before responding to Hathor.

"Mother taught us your ways. To honor and obey the gods and to be ready when the day came to face Ma'at in the Hall of Truth. I know not what my sister and I are, but I will do as my mother commanded of me and honor her—and you."

Hathor reached into the altar bowl Neema had used to summon her. She lifted the ankh and held it tightly in her hand, the ancient symbol changing at once into a single gold feather. Hathor ran her hands along the tattered cord, and it too changed into a shimmering strand. "Rise, Amani."

Amani did as she was asked, never once risking a look at Khalida. She loved her sister, but could not for the life of her understand what had gotten into her this day. Hathor placed the golden feather and chain around Amani's neck and spoke words she couldn't interrupt. When Hathor fell silent, Amani thanked her in a whisper.

Hathor then turned to face Khalida. "Why today the change, Khalida? I've watched you for years be a loving and devoted child and sister, but now, as you kneel before me, I sense rage and disdain."

"Because today the truth was brought to light. Lies spoken brought to bear, all except for one, that is. What are we?" Khalida looked between herself and Amani. "Why are we twins and yet now we are different? Why does Amani seem to have goodness in her heart and I anger? I feel nothing but pain."

Hathor nodded her head slowly. "I do not know, but I will find the answer you seek. I can tell you, though, your creation was a mistake. There have never been twin djinns born, so we all are uncertain of what to expect from you."

"Djinns?" Amani stiffened. "Mother told us stories, but we thought she was telling us of fantastic beings that didn't truly exist. Is this why all of these changes have occurred in us?"

"Yes. Today is your quarter-century birthday and the day when all djinn understand their particular talents. Yours have manifested into," Hathor paused, "well, it's still unclear. And it is the reason you will be coming with us."

"Never," Khalida spat as she moved to run. In an instant, she was but a wisp of sand and dust floating, and the next, she was trapped, with nothing but clay walls inscribed with ancient hieroglyphics and her sister to look at. "Where are we?" she hissed.

Amani wiped the tears from her eyes and straightened her shoulders. "The bronze ewer the jackal guard was holding. Thanks to you, we've been trapped. Had you held your tongue and not tried to flee, we might not be prisoners."

"Don't blame me. Blame Garai and Neema."

"I only blame you for this," Amani said as she stared at Khalida. "Hopefully, once we face our judgment, we will understand the details of who and what we are. That is, if you can manage to keep your anger under control."

Khalida started to protest, but Amani's human appearance had changed again—revealing her djinn side once more. Khalida held her tongue as Amani's sweet, delicate nature shifted dramatically to reveal her powerful djinn traits. She became something Khalida didn't recognize, but more importantly, Khalida needed to find a way to get Amani to see her point of view. If they were to be free, they'd need to work together.

"I can hear your thoughts, feel your energy, and I will do no such thing. Accept our fate, Khalida," Amani seethed.

Amani glared at her sister, and for the first time since all this happened, Khalida realized their twin bond was even stronger than it had been before. They were one being in two bodies. She pinched her arm and watched Amani react. Khalida smiled, but only for a moment before

Amani sent a blinding pain into her head, knocking her to the ground. Khalida relented and found a comfortable spot to sit inside their new prison. Thankfully, it didn't appear small in size from the inside, but instead was laid out like an open room with basic creature comforts lining the walls.

Amani, calmed and returned to her human form, ventured to the bed covered in linen, while Khalida sat at the table covered with food and drink.

Amani and Khalida spent countless hours pondering their situation. Sometimes they argued, while others they remained silent, but most were spent discussing the possibilities of exactly what they were.

"Punished for being different," Khalida would rage.

"We'll be free soon enough. They must be still watching, and these malicious outbursts of yours are only delaying our progress," Amani would retort.

Khalida started to respond, but before she could, she and Amani were turned into wisps of sand again and sent swirling into the air. When they took human form, they were standing in an elegant throne room. There before them were Ma'at, Hathor, the jackal guard, and the tattooed man. All four of them looked down at Amani and Khalida from their elevated position. Amani was in awe. The room was gilded with blue accents amidst elaborate paintings and intricate carvings of hieroglyphics. And while all of that was impressive, what amazed Amani the most was the statue of the goddess Ma'at herself, with her winged arms outstretched, the feathers adorned in bright hues, accentuating each one as if they held a special significance. Amani bowed low. Khalida, defiant as always, remained standing, but silent, at least.

"Do you know why we have brought you here?" Ma'at asked.

Khalida began to speak, but Amani interrupted. "To tell us our fate?"

"In a way, yes."

"We've made a decision regarding your future, and we hope you will see its necessity," Hathor added.

"Khaldun," Hathor pointed to the tattooed man, "will become one of your watchers. He will monitor your actions and decide if reform will be necessary."

"*May we go home?*" *Amani asked.*

"*No. We've created a place for you to dwell, but it will not be among the djinn or the humans. The djinn do not wish to have you, and you are too dangerous to be among the humans, as evidenced by the death of your parents.*"

Tears began to spill down Amani's cheeks at the thought of her mother and father.

"*We did not kill anyone. Neema killed herself and he,*" *Khalida pointed to Khaldun,* "*killed our father. We are guilty of nothing.*"

"*Hathor warned me of your indignant nature, and while I value all opinions, I do not wish to hear the words of a petulant child. You'd do well to mind your tongue.*"

Amani reached for Khalida's hand and dragged her down to her knees. "*Can you not be quiet?*" *she whispered through gritted teeth.*

"*No. If she is going to kill me, then so be it. It will be better than living out my days in a prison.*"

Hathor walked closer, the power she wielded radiating with each step she took. "*I have no need of you, Khalida, but I do value Amani. Unfortunately, your lives are bound together in an unbreakable bond. Both must live or both will die.*"

Amani gasped, and Khalida stared at her in disbelief.

"*Good. We finally have your attention,*" *Ma'at interjected.*

"*As was your mother's way, Amani, you and Khalida will live out your lives in service to Ma'at's divine rules. When the day of your judgment comes, you will hopefully greet Anubis with honor,*" *Hathor finished.*

"*The unfortunate circumstances of your creation and the actions we must take from this day forward are no fault of your own, but it is still a matter we must deal with. We've made every effort to make your new home pleasant. Thoth has calculated all you will need and has created a home capable of serving you both. It will have all the amenities you had when you lived with your parents and then some. The one condition—and it is non-negotiable,*" *Ma'at stated flatly,* "*—is that the watchers will be checking in on you often. Nothing you say or do can be withheld from them. There will be no escape, and there will be no release.*"

With tear-stained eyes, Amani replied. "*I will accept my fate and do as* you ask, but I must insist you explain to us why we are to be punished simply for being born. Who are our real parents?"

Ma'at sat motionless, but Hathor moved closer to Amani. "You and Khalida, unlike true djinn—you are different. Djinn are born of searing wind and fire, between the ranks of angels and humans. They live long lifespans, but they also die. You have free will, which is why Khalida's temper rages against the choices before her," Hathor said as she lay her hand on Amani's cheek. "Your kind can be benevolent or evil, but that is where the link between you and djinn end."

"I'm sorry, I still do not understand. Why are we so different?"

"Because your birth came out of an argument between Sekhmet and Shu. Their rage in the moment bore twin energies carrying with it traits of the god and goddess themselves, making you two extremely powerful and unpredictable. No two djinn have ever been born at the same time. When you and Khalida are together, you think the same thoughts, feel one another's pleasure and pain. Now imagine if you someday felt the rage in Khalida's heart at the same time she was feeling it. It could be the end of us all. It is a risk we cannot and will not take. I'm sorry," Hathor said with a pained smile.

Khalida's rage began to build. Amani could feel it escalating like a sandstorm. She walked away from the goddess and stood before Khalida. "This upsets me too, but your anger will kill us both. Stop now, or you will not have to wait for their wrath. I will kill us instead, ending all of this now. Everything happens for a reason, Sister. We are destined for something. Let us take this gift of life and do what we can with it," Amani pleaded.

Khalida's palms began to burn, and Amani's did, too, reminding them both just how connected they were to one another.

"Please, Sister. I do not wish to be in pain," Amani added.

"Thoth promised to find the answer to the mystery surrounding you, but until that day, this shall be your home."

The jackal guard stepped forward with a unique-looking clay vessel in hand. It was different from the previous one he held. This one was large and cylindrical, but unlike anything Amani and Khalida had ever seen. From the outside, it appeared to be two jars connected as one, but they maintained their individual shapes—like the entrance to a private chamber. Before Amani could finish taking in the jar itself, they were all transported to a stone room, with stairs leading up to a massive double door. Two alabaster guards with their arms crossed in front of them stood at the base of the steps, while paintings and hieroglyphs covered the walls and columns.

"Your home is beyond those doors. Once you enter, they will not open again," Hathor explained. "Khaldun will escort you."

The tattooed man stepped forward and moved toward Amani and Khalida. "This way," he said in a deep baritone.

Amani glanced down at where his hand was touching her and cast him a glance. He tilted his head in acknowledgment of her displeasure. He then attempted the same with Khalida, who met his eyes with an agreeable smirk. The two walked ahead, and Amani watched as Khalida seemed to be distracted by the truth of their fate. She was flirting, as she had done countless times with men their father did business with. They'd become smitten with her beauty, and she'd manipulate them to her advantage. Amani assumed Khalida was hoping she'd be able to do the same with their new watcher, but considering the look of disdain on his face, she doubted the effort would bring her sister much success.

Amani moved forward and made her way to the first step, before turning back to look at Ma'at and Hathor. After a few moments passed, she turned without another word and followed behind the watcher and Khalida. Her fate was sealed the moment she took the last step. A handful of Egyptian slaves opened the doors, and she and Khalida stepped into their destiny.

CHAPTER 12

With a gasp, the link between Amani, the Temperance card, Calla Lily, and Nathan was broken. It was as if no time had passed, and yet they were all drained from the experience. Amani's face was flushed, and her breathing was erratic just before her body went slack. Nathan leapt forward and caught her before she hit the ground.

"You don't look well. What can we do?" Calla Lily asked as she rushed to Amani's side.

"I need a moment to compose myself."

"Let me grab you some water," Calla Lily offered before running toward a sink at the back of the store.

When she returned, she handed Nathan the glass.

"Are you okay? That was some journey you took us on," Calla Lily said when Amani was sitting upright.

"I am, but it exhausted me. I've never done anything like that before." She feigned a smile. "I hope it helped."

"It did, but when you're up for it, I have a few questions," Calla Lily said.

Nathan shot her a sideways glance. He too had questions, but with the way Amani looked at the moment, he thought it would be better for her to rest. They could clear up the gray areas later.

"Or maybe we should go back to the inn and try again later," Nathan interjected.

"No, I will be fine. What is it you wish to know?"

Calla Lily paused and then blurted, "You had insight into your mother's deepest secrets. Do you have the sight?"

"No. With everything that happened that day, my mother's blood seeped into my skin, and I at once knew all of her memories—felt her every emotion. It's how I know Nathan's thoughts as well. His blood was what freed me."

"Hmm. Okayyy . . ." Calla Lily dragged out the words. "And since Khalida never touched your mother's blood, she never knew the depth of Neema's love for you both."

Amani shook her head. "And no amount of explaining would ever make her understand. She's angry. All she has ever wanted was revenge."

Calla Lily nodded her head. "She's a formidable force, from what I could see."

"Wait, so let me understand," Nathan interrupted. "Blood is the link to you being able to see a person's memories?"

"I see and feel everything," she said as she laid her hand on Nathan's cheek. "I wish I could ease the pain you are feeling with answers as to what happened to Samuel, but the only way I can tell you what happened is to have his blood or the blood of the one who had a hand in his disappearance. I'm sorry."

"We'll figure it out. For now, I'm only worried about you."

"Have you sensed Khalida since you've been free?" Calla Lily interjected.

"Yes. I felt her emotions, and I . . ." She blushed. "I think I was experiencing the connection between her and Khaldun."

"The watcher?" Calla Lily narrowed her eyes, trying to piece all this together.

"Yes, this morning before she woke, she called out his name and —" Nathan swallowed hard. "Let's just say she was in a precarious state," Nathan admitted as he helped Amani to her feet.

Calla Lily arched a brow, but from the bashful looks on both their faces, she'd use her imagination as to what they meant. "Well, this is not my expert opinion, but it is an opinion. I think you couldn't sense your sister because you were once again trapped, and now that you are free, the twin connection is working. The question remaining is what is your sister's link to this watcher."

Amani gripped her chest and cried out. "Khalida! She's near."

Calla Lily's eyes went wide. "Here in Havenwood Falls? Are you sure? We're hidden from most—even supernatural beings struggle to find us sometimes because of the magic surrounding us."

"And Khaldun is with her."

"Well, the Court is definitely going to need to know about this, then." Calla Lily sighed. "Let's get you two out of here, and I will find you later, after I have spoken with them. Don't worry. Our magic is strong. You'll be safe here."

"Thank you," Amani said. Nathan lifted her into his arms and carried her back to the inn. Calla Lily stopped to explain to Mihail, Irina, and Madame Luiza what was going on, while Nathan took Amani upstairs. There was still a lot to discover, but for now, all the two of them could do was relax and wait. Nathan laid Amani gently on the bed and covered her with the blanket. When she was comfortable, he grabbed his father's journal and began to read through it. The jars from the memory had stuck in his mind.

"Does this look familiar?" he asked, showing her the hand-drawn images.

She sat up and leaned against her arm. "Yes, but how do you have these?"

"My father drew them."

"I do not understand, Nathan. How does Samuel connect to Khalida and me?"

"If I had to venture a guess, I would say my father and his team of Egyptologists stumbled upon you by sheer accident. They were uncovering Hatshepsut's tomb, nothing more. Hathor and Ma'at's hiding place had to have been there. And based on my father's notes, you should have been safe. Your jar was sitting on a ledge with a barrier of red stones carved like scarabs and a shimmering liquid no one could identify. That, along with the mysterious hieroglyphs, should have kept most treasure hunters at bay, but for some reason, someone gambled on it being nothing more than for show." Nathan flipped through the journal and read further down the notes. "It says here the jars sat undisturbed for weeks, but one night raiders came in and stole several items from the belly of the tomb. Your vessel was broken and lay in pieces next to one of the men who tried to steal it. Apparently, his hands and face were badly burned, leaving him unrecognizable to the local workers." Nathan shrugged. "I don't understand that."

Amani shifted on the bed. "I do. I overheard the watchers talking about it once. Anyone who tried to move the jar would unknowingly awaken the protective magic surrounding us. The scarabs were made of carnelian, a powerful crystal used to protect the living and the dead. If touched, the scarabs would come to life and run into the mercury, creating a toxic combination. The person who dared to touch them would die a slow, painful death."

Nathan huffed. "Well, someone not only attempted, but succeeded in breaking the vessel, and in doing so, freed you and Khalida."

"We didn't know what happened, only that we were free. Khalida said it was our reward for good behavior." Amani paused, dropping her head. "And I believed her. I was so naïve."

"What reason would you have to doubt her? Besides, she didn't know you'd be released by human greed."

Amani sighed. "I'm not sure about that."

Nathan gave a quick shake of his head. "Why?"

"Remember when I said we met Samuel the morning we were released, and that Khalida saw a man using a box to capture people's images—said we should get one as a gift to ourselves?"

"Yes."

"And the blurred image along with the one that looked like I was standing next to someone?"

"Yeah, right here," he said, reaching for the stack on the nightstand.

"She was next to me, and the blur was her disappearing in a wisp of sand."

Realization dawned on Nathan's face, and he reached for Amani's hand. "You think she tricked you, and my father was collateral damage."

Amani nodded. "I think so. I doubt your father is alive, Nathan. I'm so sorry."

"None of this is your fault," he said as he squeezed her hand. "Khalida has a lot to answer for, but the question remains: with her close, how do we keep you safe and not susceptible to entrapment again?"

"You don't. I will keep myself safe. I'm wiser now, and my concern is for you and Calla Lily. I care for you both, and Khalida will try to use anything or anyone to get to me."

"Amani, I don't want to lose you. Yes, the circumstances of how this all came to be are insane and unbelievable, but I feel a connection with you. I . . ."

"I feel the same way, Nathan, but if I lost you after all this—after finally knowing what a life beyond my prison could be like—I would rather be dead."

Nathan caressed her cheek. "Well, if I have anything to do with it, that is not going to happen," he said before leaning down and kissing her forehead. "I want you to rest for a little bit. I'm going to go downstairs and see if Madame Luiza can make us some food," he said as he moved off the bed.

"I'll try," she replied.

WHEN THE DOOR CLICKED SHUT, Amani let her mind wander to her sister. The first weeks in their new home had been the hardest for her and Khalida, but the goddesses hadn't lied when they said Thoth had calculated all they'd need. The doors to the chamber led into an opulent palace fit for a pharaoh. It had servants and animals mingling about, with grassy knolls just beyond the gardens for the cows and chickens to graze. Sunlight and moonlight spilled onto the balconies as the days turned into night. It even had running water that fell into rectangular pools for them to either swim or bathe. They never wanted for anything. They had all the food and provisions anyone could ever need, all contained in the space of the dual vessels. They should've been happy, and they were for a time, but only having one another and the occasional visit from the watchers and Khaldun grew old quickly. Neither of them knew how long they'd live, and the infinite number of days and years hung over them like a boulder.

The pieces of the puzzle were becoming clearer to Amani after the stroll down memory lane with Nathan and Calla Lily. Khalida's flirting with Khaldun may have been innocent at first, but now Amani knew the initial manipulation must have turned into something more. Amani thought back to all the times he'd come to "check" on them. Khalida would disappear for long periods of time, but when it was happening, Amani assumed it was because she despised being watched and scrutinized by the watchers—she said she preferred to hide and avoid his questioning. How foolish she had been to think her sister was on her side.

~

"She's here. I can feel her. She's weak."

"Where?" Khaldun snarled.

Khalida waved her hand in a wide swath. "Down there somewhere. We have a connection, but it's not exact. It's still flickering for some unknown reason."

"You stay here. I'll go. I do not want you alerting her to my presence."

Khalida stood in front of him. "Actually. I think it's you who should stay. You she'd see as a threat, but me? She won't know if I'm a victim or a willing participant."

"She can sense your every emotion. She will know."

Khalida gave Khaldun a malicious grin before she dug her nails into her arm and dragged them downwards, leaving deep gouges. The open wounds began to ooze blood and the iridescent element that made her and Amani unique.

"Now hit me," she commanded.

He shook his head slowly. "There has always been something different about you, but this is taking it to the extreme, don't you think?"

"I think you're a vicious man who's kept me captive and made me his plaything for the past eighteen years, and you must be punished for your wicked ways," she teased.

Khaldun pulled her into his arms and kissed her hard and deep before biting her bottom lip. Blood dripped, and he grinned. "I'll expect you back in two days' time. If not, I will burn the town to the ground to find you, understand?"

"I do, my love," she answered before she kissed him once more. "Now hit me."

The blow Khaldun struck was hard enough to knock her out, but when Khalida came to, she was alone. She grinned. The marks on her arms were black and blue, and the blood was now dry and cakey. There was only one thing left to do—

"Amani, help me," Khalida cried out.

❧

AMANI WINCED. She could feel Khalida's pain, but decided to block her link to her twin. It was something she had learned to do a long time ago, but never told her sister was possible. Khalida's rage was too much to bear, and sometimes Amani needed a break from the link that bound them together. It became a secret she held dear and something that was only hers. When they were young girls, Amani never minded sharing things, but after the change and the truth was revealed, she didn't want to be like Khalida anymore. Amani's heart was heavy with grief, and nothing Khalida said or did felt like she even cared about Neema and Garai. True, they weren't blood relatives, but the couple had loved the sisters and cared for them unconditionally nonetheless.

The fact she and Khalida were mistakes born out of anger weighed heavily on Amani. Was their only destiny to wreak havoc on the world? Could they not be something more than what was assumed of them? Khalida truly embraced the aspects of Sekhmet, while Amani tended to have more of Shu's traits, but the truth was they transformed often. Like the tide, their emotions and personalities shifted and changed. Amani knew now, after all the time locked away with Khalida, *that* was the reason for their imprisonment. They were too unpredictable. However, Amani never enjoyed the moments when her rage rose to the surface. She may have had this power, but she never wanted to use it to harm anyone. Disconnecting her emotions from Khalida was the only hope she had of freedom from this impossible situation.

CHAPTER 13

$\mathcal{N}$athan ran into Calla Lily in the foyer of the inn. The look on her face spoke volumes.

"What's wrong?"

Calla Lily sighed. "The Court is worried. You were only supposed to be a visitor who'd be leaving in a day or two, but now, with Amani arriving unexpectedly and her sister and a watcher tracking her . . ." She paused. "It puts Havenwood Falls and all its residents in danger, and that is something they are adamantly opposed to."

"The court? Is this your judicial system here in Havenwood Falls?"

Calla Lily chuckled. "In a way. They govern the town and everything that goes on here. They have a vested interest in all visitors because they can adversely affect the balance."

"I understand, but what can we do? Where can I take Amani to be safe?"

"I don't know, Nathan. The Court members were split in regards to letting you stay and marking you with our protections. Did Amani say if she knew how close Khalida was?"

"No, but I left her upstairs to come get us some food. Maybe she'll have a better sense now."

"One of the members suggested trapping Khalida this time, thus keeping Amani safe."

"Oh sure, and how do I go about doing that?" He huffed. "I'm only human, remember? And what about this watcher? Does anyone know what he is capable of?"

Calla Lily shook her head. "No, but I do want to help you, Nathan. I want to help you both. Maybe the Luna Coven can help? Give me a little more time, and I will try to get you an answer, okay?"

"Yeah," he replied with a nervous laugh, "I doubt an hour is going to clear this up, but sure."

When Calla Lily turned to leave, Nathan made his way up the stairs with a pot of Madame Luiza's tea and some homemade biscuits and jam in hand. He hoped Amani would like it and that it would tide her over until lunch was ready. Madame Luiza said she'd bring a tray up right away. When he opened the door, he saw Amani sleeping. She looked so peaceful, and he wondered how in the world he was going to help keep her safe.

Nathan set the tray down and walked over to adjust the blanket. "All of this feels like some crazy dream, but it's become something I don't want to wake up from," he whispered. "You've gotten to me, Amani."

Nathan reached for his father's journal and went to sit in the chair across from her. He had too much on his mind to even think about resting. He read all of his father's notes—twice, in fact—but nothing stood out to him as anything he could use to help Amani. Everything here was benign, regarding the tomb and its contents, but now that Nathan knew the truth, nothing about this situation was normal. The quest to find his father's satchel had consumed him for so long that he felt off as he sat here with the truth before him. He'd lost his father a long time ago and had grieved that loss for too long, yet knowing he was truly gone was hitting Nathan hard. Amani stirred, and his heart beat a little faster. Would he end up like his father after all this was said and done? Amani was an innocent victim, but there was no doubt in Nathan's mind she had the ability to bring down entire cities if she wanted to.

"Nathan?" Amani whispered. "Are you okay? I can feel your sadness."

"I don't want you worrying about me. How are you?"

"I'm feeling much better."

"You had me worried. I didn't know how to help you or what I could do."

Amani sat up and let her legs hang over the edge of the bed, a sadness falling over her features. "From the moment you freed me from the camera, you've done nothing but take care of me. I'm so grateful for you, but I want you to know I need to leave to keep you and Calla Lily safe. I need to leave to keep everyone here in this town safe."

"You can't go alone. They'll get you for sure, and I don't want—" He stopped. "No. I will not lose you too."

"But if I stay, Khalida will use you and anyone here in Havenwood Falls against me. I think it's best to call on the goddesses and end this once and for all."

They stared at one another for a long moment. "But that will seal your fate for sure," Nathan responded.

Amani gave a faint smile. "I've never known anyone human other than my parents. You and Calla Lily have been wonderful, and I will never forget either of you."

Nathan cast his eyes to the floor. "Another impossible dream that will end in heartache," he mumbled.

Amani stood and walked over to where Nathan was sitting. She climbed into his lap and caressed his face. "If I had one wish, it would be to have you look at me every day the way you are now, but I know that is impossible."

"Why? Why can't your wish be possible? I don't want to lose you, Amani."

"You never know. Sometimes things turn in your favor. Fate has a funny way of shifting. Maybe we'll get lucky. All I know is I want to feel more of what I am feeling right now. Is that selfish?"

Nathan shook his head and then drew her mouth to his. "No," he said before he kissed her.

A knock at the door startled them both.

"That's probably our food. Madame Luiza said she'd bring it up when it was ready. Are you hungry?" Nathan asked.

Amani didn't speak. Instead she moved off of Nathan's lap and went to sit on the bed.

The smell of the food wafting from the other side of the door was a good distraction from the tension in the air. Sadness fell over Amani's features as she watched Nathan walk to the door and open it. There on a tray were two covered dishes with drinks, a white rose, and an envelope with his name scrawled on the front. Nathan brought the tray inside and set it on the dresser before reaching for the letter.

Dear Nathan and Amani,

Please eat and come downstairs when you are finished. We need to discuss a plan for the two of you to be safe. Calla Lily will be arriving with the Court of the Sun and the Moon in an hour. I hope you enjoy the meal. I added two slices of chocolate cake for you.

See you soon,
Madame Luiza

Nathan folded the letter and set it down before turning to Amani. "We have an hour before they want to meet with us."

CHAPTER 14

*N*athan and Amani made their way downstairs and came face to face with the Petran family, along with Calla Lily and nine other people. Amani tensed, and Nathan gave her hand a little squeeze. They were both caught off guard, but this was something they were going to have to do no matter what.

"Amani, Nathan, I'd like to introduce you to members of the Court of the Sun and the Moon. They are the governing body here in Havenwood Falls," Calla Lily said with a smile. "If you could please join us, we think we have a few ideas as to how to move forward."

Everyone made the proper introductions and sat at one of the larger tables in the dining room. The tension ebbed as Amani met each one of the Court members. She'd never met any other supernatural beings, and yet here before her were so many variations, all emitting an enormous amount of power as they sat in front of her and Nathan.

"What is your intention in being here?" the dark-haired mage asked with his arms crossed in front of his chest.

Calla Lily gave him a look. "Roman, we've already been over this. Amani didn't ask to be here. Neither did Nathan."

"Yet they're here and have brought their problems with them, which we now have to try to contain."

"I don't intend to be a problem. I plan on leaving. I do not wish to put Nathan and Calla Lily or anyone here in Havenwood Falls at risk," Amani interjected.

"But leaving with Khalida and Khaldun so close is not an option either," Nathan insisted. "That'll be two against one."

"We're not implying Amani should leave or face these two djinn alone, but we do have to decide how we are going to handle the safety of the town," Mihail replied.

"We received word before coming here that a woman was spotted in the woods just beyond Cooley Creek. Our belief is that this is your sister," Roman said, relaxing his posture only slightly.

"She was injured," Calla Lily added.

Amani looked at Calla Lily for a brief second before turning her attention to Roman and his visible disdain for her and Nathan.

"It's Khalida," she said coolly, "and I plan on taking care of it."

"What is your plan then?" Roman asked.

"I will handle my sister. Khaldun is not here at the moment. I cannot sense him."

"And what if he shows up?" Roman scowled.

"Then we will be there to intercede," Mihail countered. "I think all of us but you, Roman, are interested in the safety and survival of Nathan and Amani."

"Thank you," Nathan remarked, picking up on the hostility between the two men.

"That is all well and fine, but we need a plan to cover all contingencies," Roman said as he glared at Amani.

"What is your problem?" Nathan blurted.

Amani reached for Nathan's hand, turned away from Roman, and addressed the rest of the group. "I am going to go to my sister, and then we'll be leaving to meet the goddesses face to face."

"What about Nathan?" Calla Lily questioned.

Tears welled in Amani's eyes. "He understands that I have to do this to save everyone. I cannot trust Khalida, and if Khaldun does show up, kill him, because if you don't, he *will* kill you all."

A few at the table mumbled, while Roman huffed.

"We'll keep Nathan safe, Amani," Calla Lily said with tears in her own eyes. "I'm so sorry it is coming to this."

"Thank you," Amani replied. "For the small amount of time I've spent here, you mean a lot to me, and I'm grateful for all your help. I've never had a friend, but I consider you one. I will never forget you, Calla Lily."

"Oh, honey," she said as she moved to hug her.

As she did, Amani flinched and gasped in pain.

"What's wrong?" Calla Lily exclaimed.

Nathan didn't need to reach for her. He could see the agony in her eyes. It had to be Khalida. "What's wrong?"

"She's here!"

The Court members all rose at once.

"Everyone, do what needs to be done to protect the town. Saundra, alert the coven to strengthen our wards," Roman announced.

Amani's skin began to change, and previously unseen markings shimmered to life as they rose to the surface. She looked over at Nathan and mouthed "I'm sorry" just before she turned into a wisp of sand and disappeared.

CHAPTER 15

$\mathcal{A}$ ll at once, the park in town square was filled with everyone who was just sitting at the table, with one addition—Khalida. Amani stood in front, with the Court members, Nathan, and Calla Lily taking up positions behind her. Thankfully, there were not a lot of other people wandering about, but with the energy surging, Amani assumed it was the Court's doing—their way of protecting the town's people. However, Amani could not concern herself with anyone other than Khalida at the moment.

"Sister," Khalida cooed, "it is so good to see you. I thought I lost you. I came as soon as I was able to sense you."

"Yes, I am certain that was your intent. Why do you look as though you've been in a quarrel?" Amani questioned.

"Why do you look like one of them?" Khalida hissed.

"Kindness was shown to me. My clothing wasn't suitable for this time, and I was offered something new. I see you are wearing the garments of our enemies. Where have you been while I was locked away?"

"I was being held prisoner. The day we took the picture in Egypt, I lost everything—you, my freedom, everything," Khalida said as she moved a step closer.

"No, it was I who lost everything while you were indulging in the pleasures of life. Prisoner or participant?"

"I couldn't stop his desire for me."

"Your lies end here, dear sister."

"What?" Khalida feigned shock even as her hair changed from black to white—her djinn side beginning to emerge. "Why would you say that? I have suffered."

"You never were good at hiding your emotions, Khalida. Besides, I already know the truth, and the only thing I'm interested in is for you to admit it, so we can go together to face Hathor and Ma'at," Amani said, remaining calm and unchanged.

Khalida laughed. "And what is it you think you know?"

"That the only person you care about is yourself."

"Actually, I care about quite a lot, and it all revolves around my freedom. I'm not going anywhere, but you are," she said as a watcher's vessel materialized in her hand.

Now it was Amani who laughed. "I was fooled by you eighteen years ago. I won't be fooled again, and I am certainly not going to let you trap me so you may live on."

"Then I guess we are at an impasse," Khalida said before she threw the first attack.

Ironically, it was Roman who executed the counterattack, deflecting a bolt of energy away from Amani. She wasn't sure if he doubted her ability to protect herself or if he genuinely wanted to thwart Khalida. Regardless, it was then that all hell broke loose.

Several Court members were casting blows and counterblows to what Khalida was throwing at them. Amani had never seen her sister like this. The only thing she recognized in her twin was her white hair and light eyes. Everything else was a magnified version of the night their parents died and the goddesses arrived. When one of Khalida's attacks hit Nathan in the leg, Amani reacted with an attack of her own, catching Khalida off guard.

"You care for someone," she taunted when Amani rushed to Nathan's side. "Well, well."

"These innocents have nothing to do with our conflict. Leave them be," Amani ordered.

"Then come willingly, and I will leave," Khalida countered.

"I know you too well, and if I agreed to those terms, you'd still kill them to save your lies from reaching the goddesses."

Khalida barked out a laugh. "You're probably right. Humans are of no value to me," she said as she eyed Roman, "not even magical ones."

Roman was none too pleased with her insult and began to conjure a spell. Energy radiated around him, and the ground beneath Khalida shook. Amani didn't waste any time. Instead she helped Nathan to his feet, and they made their way over to a lamppost. "I'm so sorry. I should have stayed in the camera."

"Don't say that." He winced as the cut in his leg gushed blood.

Calla Lily and Madame Luiza ran to them in a rush.

"He's hurt," Amani cried.

"We've got him. Go help Roman. I'm not sure how much longer he can hold her with the way she is shimmering," Madame Luiza said as Calla Lily knelt beside Nathan.

Tears were streaming down Amani's face, but she did as Madame Luiza asked and moved opposite Roman.

"Enough, sister," Amani yelled over the din in the square.

Khalida released Roman from her attack and turned to face Amani. "Poor you, always on the other side of things. Do these humans know who you really are?"

Amani saw the members of the Court battered, but still alive. This was all her doing. She'd brought Khalida here, even if it was inadvertently. It was time to end this. She reached for the feather around her neck and pulled it to her lips.

"No," Khalida screamed and flung her hand toward Amani. The chain holding the feather began to dig into the back of Amani's neck before snapping and flying into the air. With a flick of her wrist, Amani diverted it from reaching her sister, thankful when Mihail snatched it out of midair and vanished. Khalida raged at her missed prize, and Amani was grateful her sister didn't have the necklace.

Unfortunately, it was her only means to call the goddesses—now she'd have to fight.

Amani shouted for Calla Lily and Madame Luiza to take Nathan and leave, but before they could move, Khalida shoved the women aside and grabbed Nathan. He choked and spat as her fingers wrapped around his trachea.

"Leave. Him. Alone."

Khalida leaned in to Nathan. "Let me guess, she told you she was the innocent one, and I was the one to be feared?"

Nathan couldn't speak, so he only shook his head.

"Oh, you don't believe me. Have you seen what she is? What she can do? I *had* to trap her. She's a danger to everyone."

More gasps came from Nathan, and Amani started to lose control. Her skin changed from warm caramel to steely gray as the hieroglyphs underneath turned a vibrant gold.

"Let him go or I will kill us both, Khalida," Amani seethed.

"Did you hear that? She'll kill you both," Khalida taunted Nathan before she smashed her lips against his and turned to face Amani. "Show us all who you really are, sister. Let the world see why you should be contained."

Amani's blond hair began to blow wildly around her head by a violent wind erupting from the ground beneath her feet.

"There we go," Khalida goaded. "Show them all just how evil *I* am".

Amani wasn't sure what was going to happen next. She'd never fully embraced her powers or even knew what she was capable of—she never had an occasion to, until now, but as Khalida continued to taunt her, the thoughts in her head were becoming a reality. The ground started to shake, and the sand quivered as it hovered over the grass.

"I won't ask again," Amani ordered as she struggled to control her djinn side.

Khalida laughed. "You don't even know how to be a true djinn."

Amani's resolve ended, and she let the other side of her take over. Her hair was now alight and her hieroglyphs ablaze as she sent a blast of energy at Khalida, jarring her enough that she released Nathan.

"Don't, Amani," Nathan croaked. "You'll die, too."

Khalida snarled at him, realizing he knew the truth, and moved to strike, but Amani was quicker. Unfortunately, that was when Khaldun materialized near the fountain, making it two against one.

"Time for you to come home," Khaldun snarled as his cobalt markings began to glow. Khalida and Khaldun split up, obviously hoping to strike Amani from her flank, or so she thought. Khaldun came for her, while Khalida turned back to Nathan. Mihail and Irina tried to stop Khalida, but were tossed into Madame Luiza and Calla Lily, knocking them all to the ground. Roman raged and cast a spell to protect the other Court members. It was becoming abundantly clear that all they could do was save their own, because the battle brewing between these three djinn would not end well.

Amani used the connection between her and Nathan to send him a message. *I'm sorry. I never meant to hurt you.*

Nathan didn't have a chance to respond before Khaldun tossed the watcher's vessel in front of Amani. He began to speak in a language only a djinn would recognize, an ancient tongue that sounded frightening as it was spoken. Amani turned to face him, and as the final words came out of his mouth, she seized her opportunity. Turning herself into specks of sand, she vanished. Khalida suddenly remained the only viable djinn to be trapped within the bottle. When Amani re-emerged, she remained shapeless and used this to her advantage, attacking Khaldun. He swiped at her as she swirled around him in a tornado of fiery sand. When Amani finally appeared before him, her hair was still ablaze and the gold symbols on her skin glowed as bright as the flames.

"I've always despised you, Amani. I'm going to enjoy making you suffer."

"It will not be I who suffers this day," she replied.

Khaldun laughed and lunged for her, but Amani struck with unimaginable force. Khaldun stared at her blankly, the truth of what she'd done sinking in. Amani held his beating heart in her hand, watching it as it pulsed, absent of its owner. As Khaldun dropped to his knees, Amani crushed it beneath her fingers. She knew that wouldn't be enough to finish him, so she cast her eyes in his direction, setting him ablaze. Khaldun screamed as her djinn-enhanced flames engulfed him. In a matter of seconds, he was nothing more than ash. Amani dropped his stilled heart on top of the ashes and closed her eyes, trying to quench the rage.

She heard a voice calling out to her to come back, even as her body fell limp. "It's okay. Amani, please. I'm here for you," Nathan declared. "You did it. You saved us."

She took a deep breath in and composed herself, bringing her djinn side under control. When she opened her eyes, Nathan was there before her.

"There's my girl." He smiled.

"You're okay?"

"I am."

"And Calla Lily?"

"She's fine. We're all fine."

"You saved us all, Amani," Calla Lily replied with a faint smile.

"And Khalida?"

"She's in here," Roman said, holding the vessel in the air.

"I need that," Amani declared.

"Why would I give this to you?" Roman goaded.

Amani glared at him, the golden hieroglyphs on her skin beginning to surface again in a fluid rush. "Because my kind—and my sister—are not for you to possess. Khalida belongs to the goddesses," she said coolly as she extended her hand toward him.

Roman shoved the jar into her palm. "We'll see what is mine to possess or not."

"I don't want any trouble, Roman, but if you try to thwart what is right for the sake of your desires, I will take action."

"Is that a threat?"

"No," Amani said flatly. "But understand, I would destroy this vessel before you or anyone else could possess it."

Roman continued to glare at her, clenching his jaw, as Nathan and Calla Lily stepped up next to Amani.

"Are you okay?" Calla Lily asked, casting a look at Roman.

Amani shifted her focus to Calla Lily and whispered, "Yes, but I've never fully embraced what I am before, and it frightens me a bit."

"What happens next?" Nathan asked as he held Amani's hand.

"I face the goddesses and tell them the truth of what has happened."

"But how?" Irina questioned.

Amani turned to Mihail, who'd returned to the square. "Do you have the necklace?"

"I do," he said, pulling it out of his pocket and handing it to her.

"I'm very sorry this all had to take place here in Havenwood Falls. Is the town okay?" Amani asked.

Roman relented. "The fountain may need to be replaced, but other than that, the damage is nothing a little magic can't fix."

The energy died down, and the other Court members began to make their way to where the rest of them stood.

"Now what?" Irina inquired.

"Now I ask for a favor so that I may leave your town for good."

"And what is that?" Calla Lily asked.

"When the goddesses have been called before, magic was used or a sacrifice made. I don't really have a sacrifice, so I was hoping you could help me call for them."

"You want them to come here?" Roman balked.

"Do you want us out of here or not?" Amani shot back, finding her voice.

"Fine, what do you need, then?" Roman snapped.

"This," she held up the necklace, "a copper dagger, a dove's feather, and a pile of burning embers."

Calla Lily and Nathan grinned, but Roman glared at her.

"It was what her mother used to call Hathor," Calla Lily affirmed.

"So you want us to give you these items so you can call an Egyptian goddess to the town square?"

"No, I want you to give me those items to call *two* Egyptian goddesses to the town square."

Roman's lip curled. "I'm in no mood for games."

"This is not a game. I will say my goodbyes, and then I will face my judgment," Amani said as she lifted the ewer in her hand. "We'll be leaving together."

"I'll be back in five minutes with the items you've requested," Roman said as he reluctantly turned to leave.

CHAPTER 16

*M*ihail, Irina, and Madame Luiza walked with the Court members to the fountain. From where Amani stood, they seemed as though they were plotting the best way to repair it. When she heard voices chanting, she thought, *Good, they're fixing things already.*

Calla Lily watched as Nathan and Amani stood side by side, their hands clasped, and stepped back. "I'm going to give you two a minute."

As she turned to leave, Nathan called out. "Calla Lily?"

"Yes?"

"Thank you for sending me a letter about my father's satchel. You were right. The answers you seek don't always come the way you hope."

Calla Lily's smile reached her eyes. "No, they don't."

Nathan turned to face Amani. "This trip has certainly not been what I expected."

"I'm sorry for that. I wish I had answers about Samuel."

"But that's the thing—you did give me answers. You're more than I could have ever hoped for," he said as he brought her hand to his lips. "I'll never regret getting on the train to come to Havenwood Falls, because every step has brought me straight to you."

Amani rose up on the balls of her feet and kissed Nathan.

"I have what you need," Roman's voice bellowed.

Amani blushed and squeezed Nathan's hand. "I was just saying goodbye."

She took the items Roman was handing her. "You'll need to light the sage for the embers, but everything else is there," he said as he moved to leave.

"Thank you, Roman."

"Once you do this and call on your goddesses, what protection do we need? I do not want any of the town affected."

"If you mean them no harm, no harm will come to you. It is Khalida and me they will want."

Roman gave her a clipped nod. "Then let's get on with it. The spell we cast to ward the rest of the town will be wearing off soon. No one but us needs to know what happened here."

"Very well," Amani replied.

"What can I do?" Nathan offered.

"I'd be grateful if you stayed close," Amani answered.

Nathan helped her put the items together while Roman went to talk to the rest of the Court. No one knew what was about to happen, but no matter what, it would end with Amani being gone and Nathan's heart left empty—again. *Love and loss seems to be your plight in life*, Nathan thought.

Amani closed her eyes and in a flash an altar appeared before her— her mother's altar, exactly as it had been so many centuries before. She lit the sage and waited until the smoke began to rise before laying the feather over the top. She cast a glance Nathan's way, and he tried to direct his heart and mind toward happier thoughts, since he knew she could hear and feel them. The last thing she needed right now was a distraction.

When Amani lifted the gold necklace and moved to lay it across the embers, Nathan blurted, "Can't we just keep her in there and run away? Hide for thirty or so years and then do this after we've spent a lifetime together?"

Amani shook her head and smiled. "I wish, but then I would be no better than my sister, and I don't want to be always looking over my shoulder for the watchers to come and take me away. It's no way to live. You deserve more than a life trapped within a wish, Nathan."

Nathan bowed his head. "It was worth a shot."

Amani took hold of his hand as she lay the necklace over the offering. "Hathor, I humbly request your presence, you and Ma'at. I surrender not only myself but Khalida too."

Thunder rolled, and lightning railed in the sky as the wind around them began to churn. The scent of frankincense was pungent in the air, and then sparks of fire appeared on the road in front of the nearby buildings. Four towering figures materialized before them, obscured until the fire dissipated. As they stepped forward, Amani immediately knelt, Nathan following suit, unsure of what else to do. Two larger-than-life guards with ebony skin and faces like jackals stood on either side of two elegantly dressed women, bathed in gold and jewels. Before their eyes, the two women transformed as they walked forward. They were no longer giant in size and stature, but gained more human qualities. However, their godly presence was still awe-inspiring.

"Amani?" Hathor inquired.

"Why do you summon us, and why are you here?" Ma'at asked before she surveyed the area.

"Khalida and I were freed for a time, but then she and Khaldun trapped me in a camera, where I remained a prisoner for the past eighteen years," Amani answered quickly.

"And where are they now?" Hathor thundered.

Amani bowed her head and held out the ewer. "Khalida is in here, and Khaldun is dead."

"I see," Ma'at acknowledged. "Your doing?"

"Yes."

Hathor walked over to Amani and took the bronze vessel from her outstretched hands. "And who is this?" the goddess asked, turning her attention to Nathan.

"This is the man who freed me from the camera and Khalida's betrayal," Amani said as she offered her hands to Hathor and Ma'at. "See for yourself."

They took her hands, and Amani sent images of the past eighteen years into their minds.

"Nathan and the people here are all innocent. I humbly ask your forgiveness and beg to have this wrong righted," Amani said as the last image faded.

"And what is it that you wish for us to do?" Ma'at asked.

Amani steeled her gaze. "Erase any trace of this from their minds. Make it so they will be spared the pain of what has come to pass by no fault of their own."

"No, Amani," Nathan pleaded.

"I can feel the sorrow in your heart, Nathan." Amani lifted her eyes to meet his. "And I do not want you to pine for me once I am gone. You must live your life and be happy."

"I'm happy now."

"You've spent eighteen years searching for answers to your father's disappearance. I was tied to those answers." She gently touched his face. "You deserve more."

"I deserve you."

"Amani," Hathor interrupted, "who is the male to you?"

Amani turned to face Hathor. "Someone I care about very much. He saved me and in turn saved himself, along with the people behind me. The woman there," she pointed to Calla Lily, "she too helped me see the truth. I'm indebted to them both."

Ma'at turned toward Calla Lily and the Court. "And you? What do you say about what happened this night?"

Mihail stepped forward. "Amani did as she said. Her sister came to kill us all, and the watcher was with her. If not for Amani, we'd all be having a very different conversation."

"But is she not the reason Khalida and Khaldun came in the first place?" Ma'at questioned.

"From what I understand, that was not by her doing," Mihail replied.

"And this camera, how did it come to be here in your town?" Hathor asked.

Calla Lily stepped next to Mihail. "The simple answer—magical intervention. One day it simply appeared in my shop, and I contacted the person I believed to be its owner. Nathan responded to my inquiry, and the rest is history," she affirmed.

Hathor looked back to where Amani and Nathan were standing. "I am pleased. You did as I knew you would. The good in your heart won out over the wrath. Khalida never could see the truth of her existence and how she could change it."

"I'm not sure I am ready to declare judgment," Ma'at said flatly. "Instead I propose an offer." She paused. "Will you accept Amani as a temporary resident here in your home until we can confer with Thoth on the path we should take?"

Roman started to speak, but Saundra Beaumont answered instead. "We will gladly accept Amani and Nathan into Havenwood Falls. It is clear her intentions are only to help and not harm. It was not that long ago that our ancestors were faced with an unimaginable choice, and they too needed guidance to proceed."

Amani gasped, and Nathan stood silent.

Ma'at gave a gracious nod to the woman with the silvery white hair before she walked back over to Hathor. "We will send word when we are due to return. In the meantime," she said as she waved a hand over the square, "let your town be cleansed."

A golden-hued smoke wafted over the open space, clearing it of all trace of the battle that had raged. As the air cleared, four flames emerged, and the jackal guards, along with Hathor and Ma'at, stepped into the vermilion glow, disappearing into thin air.

Nathan pulled Amani into his arms, and Calla Lily ran to them. "Well, it seems we'll need to find you a place to stay, since you'll be here in Havenwood Falls for a bit."

"You're more than welcome to stay in one of the rooms at the inn, if you'd like," Irina added.

Amani turned to Saundra, Mihail, Roman, and the rest of the Court, and bowed. "Thank you. I will honor this gift, and if I can in any way help you, I am at your service."

"Where is the ewer and Khalida?" Roman interjected.

"Safe where she belongs," she met his eyes, "with the goddesses."

"I certainly hope so," he said with disdain as he turned to walk away.

"We're happy to have you both. Come to see me tomorrow, so we can officially register you for your stay here in Havenwood Falls," Saundra smiled.

"Stop by the store too, and I'll help you shop for some more clothes," Calla Lily added.

With that, they all turned to go, leaving only Amani and Nathan in the square.

"Now what?" Nathan grinned.

Amani looked into his eyes. "One step at a time."

"One step at a time, then," he said as he leaned down and placed a kiss on her lips.

Continue Amani and Nathan's journey in *Released From a Curse*.

We hope you enjoyed this story in the Legends of Havenwood Falls series featuring a variety of supernatural creatures. The series is a collaborative effort by multiple authors.

Lost in Time by Tish Thawer
Dawn of the Witch Hunters by Morgan Wylie
Redemption's End by Eric R. Asher
Trapped Within a Wish by Brynn Myers
Blood and Damnation by Belinda Boring
Fated Beginnings by E.J. Fechenda
Emeline by Katie M. John
Released From a Curse by Brynn Myers
A Pack of Lies by Kallie Ross
Kiss the Ashes by Desiree Lafawn
Hidden Truths by Colleen Nye
Wrath and Retribution by Belinda Boring
Changing Fate by Char Webster

Rise of the Witch Hunters by Morgan Wylie
The Drowning Bride by Seven Jane

Also try the main Havenwood Falls series; the YA line, Havenwood Falls High; the darker, sexier side of town, Havenwood Falls Sin & Silk; and the local supernatural college, Sun & Moon Academy.

Stay up to date at www.HavenwoodFalls.com

Subscribe to our reader group and receive free stories and more!

ABOUT THE AUTHOR

Brynn Myers is an adult paranormal romance author. After considering writing a hobby for years, she finally turned her passion and talent into a career. She came into the paranormal genre later than most, but has always loved fairy tales and all things magical. Using that love, she creates charmed worlds by writing stories involving passionate, strong-willed characters with something to discover.

You can find out more about Brynn and her all titles by visiting www.brynnmyers.com and subscribing to her newsletter at www.brynnmyers.com/subscribe.

ACKNOWLEDGMENTS

I'd like to thank Ang'dora Publishing for asking me to be a part of the Havenwood Falls crew. I am thrilled to have had the opportunity to write in the Legends series. I'd also like to give a special thanks to Kristie Cook for allowing me to reference her characters, and to Randi Cooley Wilson for letting me roll with Calla Lily Mircea and Roman Bishop. It was my honor, and I hope I did them all justice.

Much love to my own publisher Amber Leaf Publishing. Thank you always for your love and support in all my work. I will never be able to thank you enough.

To my readers and anyone new to www.brynnmyers.com — THANK YOU!! Every time you pick up one of my stories and give my characters a chance to warm your hearts or royally tick you off, I AM BLESSED! Thank you for making this fantastic ride worth it with all your love and kudos! Much love to you all!

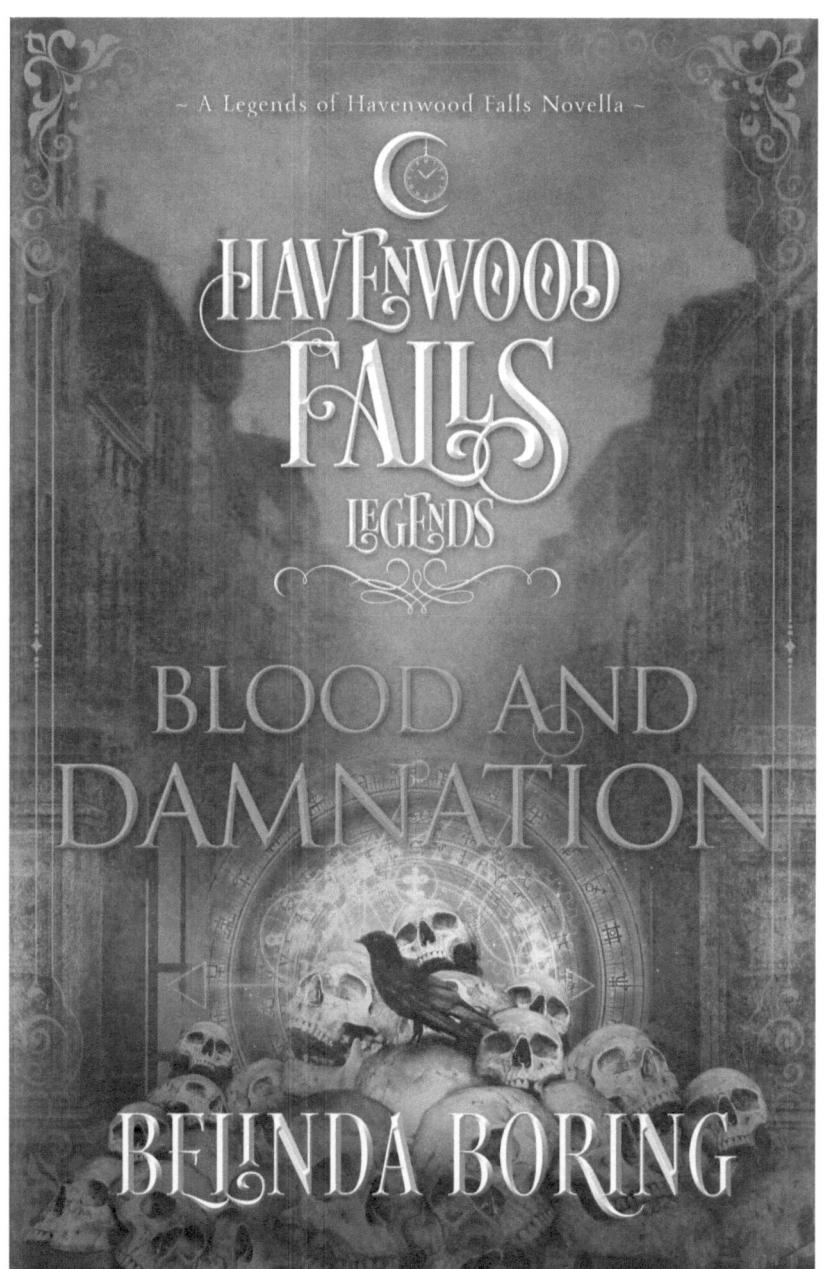

~ A Legends of Havenwood Falls Novella ~

HAVENWOOD FALLS

LEGENDS

BLOOD AND DAMNATION

BELINDA BORING

Blood and Damnation (A Legends of Havenwood Falls Novella) by Belinda Boring

With the world laid out before him, Marcus St. James enjoyed the many fruits of society, none more so than the women who fell at his feet and lifted their skirts. A few whispered promises and he could have whichever beauty caught his eye. Until the night he led a young gypsy woman into the alleyway, where more than just heated kisses were exchanged.

Knocked unconscious, Marcus awakens to find his companion dead in his arms, her blood screaming for justice. Before he can uncover the truth, her family arrives—hellbent on punishing the person who murdered their kin. Ignoring his pleas of innocence, they curse him to an existence as a blood drinker.

In the wake of death, a new purpose is born, transforming Marcus into a monster. Driven by his thirst for vengeance, he focuses on hunting down the gypsies who destroyed his life. But when an innocent girl finds her way into his fortress, Marcus must decide what the true curse is: a life filled with blood and damnation or one void of love and hope. He'll discover one lasting truth—love can soften even the hardest of hearts. And can also stoke the fires of retribution.

BLOOD AND DAMNATION

AN EXCERPT

1868

Blood.

It was everywhere.

There wasn't a place I could lay my hand that didn't come back covered. As I lifted my fingers to my brow, the fading sun caused the redness of the liquid to take on an even more sinister hue.

As if being bathed in blood could get more sinister, I chuckled silently.

There really wasn't anything funny about the situation, but for the life of me, I couldn't stop the wave of hysteria that threatened to overcome my sensibilities. It started somewhere in the base of my chest and rose with such force that to ignore it, to stifle it, would cause more pain than it was worth.

So I let it out.

Ripples of laughter echoed in my ears—sounding completely foreign and unhinged.

I shuddered to think what would happen should someone stumble by and find us like this. I imagined I would look like a madman sitting in the middle of a dirty, rat-infested alley, quietly cradling the lifeless body of a woman in his arms.

They may have witnessed the precise moment her heart stopped—the last of her lifeblood trickling slowly from her wounds.

I knew I looked disheveled, my clothes caked with blood that was already beginning to dry, my exposed skin smeared with the sticky gore. I also knew that people would not stop to ask questions. Instead, they would run screaming for the authorities.

Sounds slowly filtered back into my awareness, and the abrupt slap of reality returned me to my senses. My bloodstained hands roughly smoothed over fine black hair as if to comfort her in death.

My victim, I thought without hesitation.

I had somehow done this. Bile bubbled up into my mouth while I observed my gruesome surroundings, the bitter scent of copper made me gag, and numbness spread through me, shock wrapping its icy fingers around my heart.

I turned the woman's face so her lifeless eyes stared back at me, as if in death she continued to accuse me. Her name had been Primrose, or was it simply Rosa? Letting out a hasty breath, I cursed my stupidity for not remembering her name.

Whoever she was, she had been beautiful, her skin still holding a slight warmth from being held so close.

She'd caught my eye earlier in the evening as I strolled through the crowds attending the annual town fair. With her long raven-colored tresses and green twinkling eyes, I'd spent the better half of the evening exchanging glances and sensual flirtations.

London gossiped about my "rakish" ways. I had a useful talent of layering my seductive charms on so thick that it always guaranteed me getting what I wanted—whoever I wanted. My goal was that before the night was over, she'd be beneath me, writhing as I drew out every ounce of pleasure within her.

She'd responded so freely to my suggestions that it wasn't long before she'd led me to this very alley, secluded from prying eyes. I'd immediately pressed her up against the wall as my mouth devoured hers.

Her eagerness had stoked a fire in me. Gone was the frigidity I often met from my own fellow countrywomen, and my urgency was met with her own brand of fire.

With each caress, each flick of her tongue, she sent me careening out of control. When she'd softly moaned over my touching her covered breast, I'd instinctively deepened our passionate kiss.

She'd tasted of mead and sunshine.

Even now, the thought of that fevered kiss made my mouth water.

She'd felt so good and responded so well to my attentions that I'd lost track of time. One moment she was racing toward release and the next she was lying in my arms.

Dead.

I frowned, my mind desperately trying to piece the events together, but all I could sense was an oppressive fog—one that was unwilling to succumb to my frantic probing.

Something had happened, but still it remained elusive.

Shock wouldn't hold it from me forever.

Moments passed, and more sounds filled the night air.

"They'll discover us soon," I murmured, still unable to do anything but stare down at the woman who had previously set my entire body aflame.

My skin pebbled from the chill now settling over me. The sweat clinging to my once pristine shirt caused a slight tremble to begin.

Where was my coat?

My hands slowly released her, and that's when I discovered I'd taken it off to cover Rosa.

Primrose?

The body.

Muscles groaned from suddenly being forced to move, and I gingerly pushed the weight from my lap, careful to not disturb the woman further. This caused another chuckle to erupt.

The time for gentleness and consideration had passed with her last breath, but still I couldn't bring myself to think of her as dead. It felt wiser for my dwindling sanity to consider her asleep, and as if to prove that point, I leaned over one more time and tentatively laid my lips to her cool forehead for one last kiss.

My lips came back wet, no doubt glistening from her blood.

That was all the truth and reality I needed.

As my resolve snapped, I toppled to the side and began violently heaving.

"Dear God," I groaned, too weak to wipe at my mouth.

The feeble contents of my stomach mingled with the drying pool of blood as if taunting me, forming a macabre mixture.

The smells of the alley—the smell of her—assaulted my senses again, driving me to purge my stomach until all that was left was a repeated gag.

I gasped for air, my chest struggling to drag in enough oxygen to compensate for the violence. My stomach screamed from my muscles being roughly contracted.

It took everything I had to stand, staggering slightly as the world began to spin. Unable to take my eyes away from the body, I suddenly realized that I'd lingered too long.

With the alley open at both ends, a channel between two streets, it was only a matter of time before someone else would seek to use it. I had to flee. I couldn't be found here . . . not like this.

I'd made it a mere two steps before a hysterical shriek pierced the air.

Panic blasted through me as the scream evolved into guttural sobbing, revealing two strangers. One of the women threw herself to the ground and scooped Primrose up into her arms, pinning the now stiff body to her chest. Tears cascaded down her wrinkled cheeks.

Words flew out of the older woman's mouth in short spurts of some foreign language, one that sounded familiar. She wore a haunted expression, her hands frantically searching over the person I assumed was someone she knew and loved.

She was feeling for the fatal wound.

I stood transfixed, held tightly by the women's grief. Chivalry screamed for me to go comfort her, but even I knew how badly this appeared. Her loved one was dead and there I stood—smeared with her blood.

The other woman, much younger in appearance, maybe a sister or cousin, finally reached the spot of despair and flung her arms around the rocking figure. She added her sobs to the melee, and something within me jolted.

I shouldn't be watching this. This was too private, too intimate, and it wasn't for me to witness.

My traitorous foot crunched on discarded litter as I took a step away. The movement caused the air to suddenly silence as two pairs of tear-filled eyes snapped on me.

Anguished.

Wretched.

Furious.

Frozen by the honesty I couldn't ignore, I willed myself to move, to break contact with the piercing gazes that scrutinized me. It wasn't difficult to read the judgment filling their faces. They took everything in—my appearance, the blood, what I assumed was my guilt-stricken expression.

The younger woman gasped as she made the sign of the cross, her hands trembling with strong emotion. Even though she was at a distance, the word *mulo* reached my ears.

Death.

That word. I knew it. It meant death.

Pieces clicked together as my brief lover's face flashed through my mind. Primrose had been my escort for the evening. I would've recognized her heritage, had I not been so fixated on bedding her.

Guilt. Waves of guilt pulsed through my veins as memories finally surfaced.

The spell that held me broke, and without thinking, I stepped forward, moving toward the women with my hands outstretched in a sign of submission. There was no denying my sense of survival begged me to run, but honor compelled me to stay. There were explanations to be made, questions to be answered, and somewhere amongst the emotions churning thickly in the air, I hoped to uncover some of my own.

Evidence be damned. I couldn't have done this. My lust ran toward the flesh and losing myself between a pair of willingly spread legs. It wasn't in death, murder, and violence.

It was with these thoughts that my confidence slowly strengthened. Romani people were often present on my family's estate when I was growing up. I'd spent many a childhood summer running and playing with the children of different traveling families, so dealing with the two women wouldn't pose too difficult a problem.

"Hello." My voice croaked from being unused.

Angry stares answered. Neither woman spoke, which caused me to stop mid-step.

Perhaps I'd underestimated the situation. How could this be resolved if they refused to acknowledge me?

I did the only thing I knew to do—I tilted my head forward in a respectful bow. We English prided ourselves on having impeccable manners.

With a scratchy throat and my mouth feeling as though I was trying to swallow fireplace ash, I tried again. For a brief second, I wished I had a tankard of mead, anything that would help so I could make this speech and leave.

I took in a deep breath, and thankfully my voice didn't hold the weakness from before. I sounded strong, diplomatic, trustworthy even.

"My name is Marcus. Lord Marcus St. James of Smithersby Field . . ."

A cold tone interrupted my friendly introduction.

"We know who you are." It was the older woman, the grandmother, if I'd judged correctly, who spoke. She then punctuated her statement with a sharp noise as she spat on the ground angrily.

"We know exactly who you are. *Chor.*"

My brow crinkled as I hurriedly tried to translate the foreign word. Something tugged at a distant memory. I was sure I'd heard it before, but the stress of the evening was causing me to draw an annoying blank.

"I'm sorry. I don't know what that word means," I mumbled in response.

Again, the woman interrupted.

"*CHOR.*" The word rang out with a blistering force as her finger shot out, pointing straight at me. Accusation and hatred exploded across her face.

There was no withstanding the vehemence of her verbal attack. Stuttering, struggling to find a way to placate her, all I could do was stand there—speechless. For the life of me, I had no idea what she was saying.

"She's calling you a thief," the grief-stricken voice of the younger female revealed. She must've been a few years older than Primrose.

"I assure you, I am no thief. Allow me to say again . . . my name is Marcus St. James. Believe me, there's an explanation for this. This is not what it seems."

"It matters not what your name is. It's your actions that label you a thief. You stand there covered in the blood of our beloved, hoping to slip away into the night after stealing the life of sweet Primrose. You are a thief, a black-hearted stealer of innocence."

"Please, let me continue." I took another step forward. "I didn't do this. I didn't kill her. I'm not quite sure what happened. One moment we were becoming . . . *acquainted*, and then she was dead."

The moment it passed through my lips, I knew how dubious and feeble my explanation sounded. Even the most uneducated of commoners could poke a hole through it with enough certainty to convict and then hang me.

"What do you mean *acquainted*?" The question thundered brashly in the alley.

My face flushed, and I tried loosening the tightness of my shirt collar, only to find blood flaking away when I pulled my fingers back. The small pieces fluttered to the ground, some snagging the thigh of my trousers. Repulsed, I jerked violently as I tried to brush them away.

Some would say it was a compelling act of guilt—the killer unable to face the truths of his sins.

Everywhere I looked, I saw blood. *Her* blood. In some places it was so thick, it caused my clothing to stick and dry to my skin.

I gagged again, quickly covering my mouth. This wasn't a moment to show weakness, but there was no helping it. With each passing breath, my hope of escaping this nightmare grew dimmer.

"What do you mean *acquainted?*" the woman repeated. "Do you mean to stand there and say that not only did you murder my sister, but you also corrupted her with your debauched and vile ways?" Her gaze narrowed on me as if she'd already judged and condemned me.

Images from earlier returned to invade my mind.

Primrose squirming against me, her hand rubbing hard against my erection. Based on her nymph-like response, she'd definitely been corrupted, but not by me.

If there was even an inkling of possibility that they'd believe me, I would tell that to her family. I would give them a quick education on how very *unvirtuous* their precious Primrose was.

The older woman drew herself up slowly, finally coming to a stand. She'd been quietly rocking back and forth with the deceased as she watched the interaction between her kinswoman and me. She was small, as women went, the years beginning to hunch her over with a stoop. I would've sworn that as she stood there, vengeance blazing in her eyes, she grew in stature—rivaling my own height.

"*Chor!*" she accused. As she stepped around the body she'd lovingly been holding, an energy began to fill the space around them. Somewhere in the distance, I heard dogs howling as thunder shook the air. Something was stirring, and it felt as though its focal point was solely on me.

The words were coming thick and fast as the woman launched into a rhythmic speech that was occasionally broken up by her quick gasps for breath. She droned on and on for what seemed like a lifetime.

I was able to pick out the occasional word, but what I heard next chilled me to the core.

Bibaxt. Bad luck.

Marime. Outcast.

Naswalemos. Sickness.

Strazhno. Danger.

Amria. Curse.

That word hit me the hardest. She was cursing me, and as I

propelled myself forward to stop her, a pain like nothing I had *ever* experienced drove me abruptly to my knees with a demonic roar of agony.

Fire blazed through my veins, heating then boiling my blood until I was positive my insides were liquefying. Sweat dripped from every pore as my body trembled with vicious convulsions that threatened to render me insane.

Now writhing on the floor, words failed me.

All I could see—feel—was excruciating pain.

Deep within my chest a humming began, the sensation causing my heart to beat erratically. All I wanted to do was beg for death as I felt something inside me explode. Whether from mercy or approaching unconsciousness, the pain began to fade as everything dulled. My vision darkened.

I wept with relief. As I curled up into a ball so I could welcome oblivion like a long-lost friend, a single word reached out and branded my soul.

Shilmulo.

A small shard of alarm pierced me the moment I recognized it, but I was without hope, the world finally crashing around me.

Shilmulo.

Vampire.

Purchase *Blood and Damnation* where books are sold.

www.ingramcontent.com/pod-product-compliance
Lightning Source LLC
Chambersburg PA
CBHW052009170626
46808CB00007B/2842